Tab

Chapter 1 1
Chapter 2 6
Chapter 3 17
Chapter 4 25
Chapter 5 34
Chapter 6 43
Chapter 7 53
Chapter 8 60

© Copyright 2019 by Van Cole All rights reserved.

In no way is it legal to reproduce, duplicate, or transmit any part of this document in either electronic means or in printed format. Recording of this publication is strictly prohibited and any storage of this document is not allowed unless with written permission from the publisher. All rights reserved.

Respective authors own all copyrights not held by the publisher.

My Soldier
MM Best Friend Romance

By: Van Cole

Foreword

I returned from the war with scars that run deeper than my flesh. Tormented by memories of the past I wonder if I'll ever be able to become the man I used to be, or if I'm always destined to be this shell that returned from the foreign country, broken and battered and defeated.

There seems to be little hope for improvement until I receive a surprising call from my old best friend, Clint. We lost touch a while ago as life took its hold on us, but as we reconnect, I start to remember why he was such a good friend. He's the only one who can get me to talk about my emotions, and as I open up to him, I start to feel something else. Something unfamiliar…something a little scary, but very exciting.

Maybe, just maybe, we can save each other.

My Soldier

Chapter 1

The air was dry and hot. Sweat prickled on my skin. My gear weighed heavily on me, like solid weights. I looked up, but the glare of the sun blinded me. Bullets cracked through the air. I yelped and whimpered like a little lost puppy. Fear gripped my heart. Sand filled my mouth, and I coughed. I was in a foreign desert, a backwater place far from home, defending my country. An explosion bloomed in the distance, a plume of smoke rising through the air, followed by an orange supernova. I turned and rolled over. I heard the cries of all my friends, my allies, the people who had come to mean so much to me. I heard them cry out in pain. I saw them fall to the floor, clutching their guts and their wounds. I watched blood spill out over the golden sand as all the armor and gear we wore did nothing. We were nothing compared to the little shards of metal slicing through our flesh.

I clung to the ground as if it offered life itself. I buried my head in the sand, literally, just waiting for it all to be over. I was a soldier. I was a brave man, defending his country from the enemy, protecting the people back home, except they had no idea what I was doing. Nobody did, except the men and women who were dying around me.

I heard them all fall to the ground, and I just stayed there, shaking. I tried so hard to will myself to pick up the gun, but my hands wouldn't move. I was paralyzed. I clamped my eyes shut and tasted the salty tears that trickled down my face, leaving tracks through the dry sand. I was sure that one of the bullets would have my name on it, that one of them would end me just like all my friends.

But then the bullets stopped. The thunder in the air settled. I heard a car drive away, the triumphant whoops and hollers of the natives fading into the distance. The glare of the sun beat down upon me as

I tentatively lifted my head and looked around at the carnage. Dead bodies lay all around me, wounded people groaned and moaned, writhing in agony, and I was laying there, unharmed, my gun unused. I was a disgrace to my uniform, to my country, to my friends. I had been sent there to defend and protect, but all I could do was cower in the dirt and the sand, praying for it all to be over.

It wasn't over for another few months. Somehow I managed to make it to the end of my tour without anyone looking at me like I was a coward. They all told me I was brave for making it through, that I had done my country proud, but I knew different. I knew I was just a lucky son of a bitch who should have been killed with a thousand other men. I was a disgrace, and something inside me broke that day, something in my mind snapped, and I wasn't sure I was ever going to be the man I used to be.

Even now I wake up in cold sweats at night, and it's been a couple of years since I returned home. Somehow it has to end, hasn't it? God, I hope so. I pray every day for salvation, even though I don't really think I deserve it. Maybe this is my penance for surviving when so many other, worthier people didn't. Maybe this is just what I deserve.

I drank the water beside my bed and looked out at the dawn sun rising through the window. It had been another night where my dreams were plagued by the sounds of bullets and explosions, the cries of victory as I looked around at my wounded friends. The worst part was that the war was still going on. Somehow despite all the sacrifice and all the death, we hadn't achieved anything. I had sold my soul to the army, and all I'd been given in return was a plague.

I pulled myself out of bed and staggered downstairs, ignoring the glittering decorations around the house.

"Morning, Bobby," Mom said. She wore a cheery smile. I felt worse for her more than anything. She'd lost so much already. I was all she had left, and I was just a shell of the boy I used to be. Sometimes at night, when she thought I was asleep, I'd hear her on the phone to her friends talking about how I wasn't the same as I used to be and how she hated the government for taking her little boy away from her. I wished I could be the same, I wished I could go back to being the way I was, but I was different. I just couldn't come to terms with the man I had turned into. It felt as though I had been corrupted, and my innocence had been stolen away. Once gone, it could never return.

I grunted at her in reply. She didn't deserve it, but somehow, I couldn't stop myself.

"What are you going to do today, dear?" she placed a plate of pancakes in front of me. I chewed on them. Even they didn't taste the same as they used to. Nothing did. All I tasted when I ate was the dry sand of the desert.

"Probably go for a run and then go to the gym."

"Why don't you go to the library instead? You always used to like reading. It would be good for you to get another hobby, it must get so boring doing the same thing at the gym all the time."

"It helps me relax."

"I did hear there's a group that meets there as well today. I can go with you if you like," she suggested, her voice faltering.

"I don't need a group, Mom. I don't need to talk about anything." I looked down at the bowl of cereal, trying to block out the world, trying to block out her. Every time I spoke to her, I was filled with guilt because I just couldn't seem to stop snapping at her with everything I said, even though I knew she didn't deserve it. I just wished that everyone could leave me alone, wished that the world would go away so people wouldn't try to make me feel better. Didn't they realize that I just couldn't feel better?

I finished up breakfast. Mom stayed in the kitchen, filling the void with an emotional silence that was tense and uncomfortable. Sometimes I felt like a ghost, walking through life while other people were trying to talk to me, and all I wanted was to be left alone. I hated the burden of trying to find a job, trying to contribute to society when

I'd already given everything I had, but nobody seemed to care. Mom pitied me, but I could tell that she was frustrated as well, wanting to get me out of the house. I was a grown man. I shouldn't still be living with my her, but I had nowhere else to go, and that only added to the guilt, knowing that I couldn't repay her, knowing that I couldn't ever thank her properly for all she had done for me. I felt worse with each day that passed. Every time I looked at her I knew, that she wasn't looking back at the son she wanted. She wanted someone healthy, someone who had friends, a relationship, someone who she could be proud of. Instead, she ended up with me.

"I'll see you when I get home," I said before I left. She called out a goodbye, but I didn't bother to look at her. I grabbed my gym bag and threw it in the truck, then pulled away from the house. I turned on the radio, trying to find some station that would play some good old fashioned music, but everything now was a load of crap, and I wondered why we even bothered defending this country when everything was vapid and shallow. I gripped the wheel, and as I looked around at the world, I grew increasingly annoyed. There were kids in nearby cars who were fooling around, people wandering about the streets lost in their own world, and decrepit buildings falling apart. This was supposed to be the apex of civilization, but it just seemed like any other place in the world, slowly degrading and crumbling away. Soon it would all be dust anyway. That's all any of us would ever be, just dust in the wind.

As I drove along, I let my mind wander and thought about the modern horrors of the world when suddenly I hit a pothole. The truck dipped and lurched, and instinctively I twisted the wheel to avoid it, but in my mind, it wasn't a pothole, it was a mine. I swerved dramatically. The wheels screeched as I hit the brakes and the truck spun and hit the curb, my body jerked, and I gazed back, feeling stupid because all I saw was an empty road with a dumb pothole, but in that instant in my mind it had been as real as the mines that exploded back when I was in the army. I could almost smell the rising heat in the air and taste the dust in the back of my throat. My heart raced, and I gripped the wheel so tightly that my knuckles were white.

A couple of cars passed along and honked at me as they swerved out of their lanes to dodge the rear of my truck. I composed myself and reversed out, then continued on my way to the gym, feeling stupid that my mind was so weak. I knew that I wasn't in the army anymore, that I wasn't in that stupid desert, yet somehow I still thought I was. I hated how my mind betrayed me, and continued to betray me even though I had been home for a while.

Was I ever going to be able to escape this damned mental hell?

Chapter 2

I managed to make it to the gym without any further incident. I wore a scowl as I strode into the gym and prepared for my workout. It was the middle of the day, so the gym was pretty empty; most people were at work, living worthwhile lives where they contributed to society. People like me were stuck here, each of us glowering, hating our lives, wishing that we could do better. I saw signs for the meeting that Mom had mentioned and turned my gaze away. What good did talking ever do anyone?

I went to the treadmill first for a little cardio and stomped my feet on the moving conveyor belt, upping the speed to push my body to its limits. Sweat prickled my brow and made my clothes cling to my skin. I didn't bother watching television or listening to music. I just focused my gaze ahead and tried not to think of anything. Running was good for that. It let me switch off my mind and lose my thoughts. It was basically the only time when I was able to let go of the terrors tormenting my mind. Even when I was asleep, I didn't have a chance to relax. I ran as fast and as hard as I could, as though I was trying to outrun the demons that were chasing me. I could feel the treadmill shake under the weight of my feet, could hear the grunts that emerged from my mouth. In my peripheral vision I caught the images of talk show hosts chattering on about meaningless things, I saw other people wandering about the gym, I blinked the sweat out of my eyes and I wished that I could just run forever.

Then it hit me, I was running as hard and as fast as I could, but I wasn't getting anywhere. I slowed and hopped off the treadmill, hanging my head. It was like a metaphor for my life. I was trying my hardest, letting sweat drip off my head as I pushed my body to the limit, but I still wasn't making any progress. I wiped my face with a towel and felt the vigor and strength coursing through my body. I needed more, needed to do more to get rid of all this anger and energy inside me. I walked over to the weights and started to pump some iron, watching my muscles glisten as I tortured myself by heaving heavy weights up in the air. I was punishing myself, just like I had been punished in the army with all of its rigorous training.

I carried on until my muscles were burning, and my mind was crying out for relief. I gulped down some water and looked down at my body, disgusted by what I saw. I was a weapon that had been made by the United States Army. I had been forged in heat and gunfire, and now I was a weapon without a use. What good was it being in prime physical condition if I had no reason to be? I needed a purpose, I needed some meaning to my life, but I had no idea where to find it. What was the use of being a soldier if there was no war to fight? I looked around, trying to see if there was anyone who needed protecting, but there wasn't. Everyone was safe. Everyone except me, it seemed.

I went back to the locker room and had a shower, washing away the sweat and grime that made my body slick. The warm water sloshed down my toned physique and helped calm the ache in my muscles. I stayed in there for a long time, letting the steam and the sizzle of the water drown out my thoughts, not wanting to leave. Where was I supposed to go? What was I supposed to do? I could drive around for a bit because I didn't want to go home. I couldn't take facing Mom again. I was a worthless piece of shit who had nothing to his life. I couldn't get a job. It was as though the world had passed me by, had moved on while I had been away and didn't care at all that I was back.

Before I knew it, I was sobbing. I hung my head and felt the tears trickle down my cheeks. Thankfully they got lost in the water, so I didn't have to be ashamed. I was alone in the shower, as well. It wasn't the first time I had cried since I'd been home, and I doubted it would be the last. It was stupid, really. I never used to cry, not because I thought it wasn't manly or anything, I just never had the need to. I used to feel sad and lonely, but crying? It seemed like an extreme reaction. But this was different. The emotions were overwhelming, and apparently my body didn't know any other way to handle them. My body shuddered and shook as I wept until I heard the locker room door open. I sniffed back my tears and wiped my eyes and decided that it was time to leave.

    I nodded to the men, wondering if they noticed how raw and red my eyes were. I dried myself and put on some clean clothes, wishing that I felt better. Even the natural endorphins that were released through exercise weren't enough to soothe the aching sadness that throbbed within me. It was like I didn't know how to feel anything but depressed.

    I grabbed my bag and walked out of the gym, trying to decide where to go next. I didn't have much money, so there was no point in going to the mall just to torture myself by looking at all the things I couldn't afford. This was galling in and of itself because I knew a lot of people working menial jobs who treated themselves to all the latest luxury items. I had literally put my life on the line, and the most luxury I could afford was to buy the occasional Subway sandwich.

    As I walked out of the locker room, I looked down the hallway to see an open door, and I heard voices. It was the meeting of the veterans. I gulped, pausing, wondering if I should go and pay them a visit. I walked towards the door, but stopped outside, leaning against the wall, listening to the man speaking.

    "When I came back, I was welcomed with open arms by my family and my girl, and that first night I thought everything was going to be alright. I was home, and we had a good meal and watched some TV, and then I got into bed, and I went to make love to my girl and I just...I just couldn't. I didn't know why. I was supposed to be a man, you know? She'd waited for me, and I'd waited for her, and my body wanted it but my mind...my mind just wanted something else entirely. I didn't know what was wrong. She told me it was okay; that I was just tired from all the traveling, but I knew something was different. I was different. Everything changed, and I couldn't enjoy the things that I'd been fighting to defend. Even the food tasted different. Eventually, my girl left me and I just...it felt like I'd lost everything."

The man sobbed, and I was struck by how much I identified with what he was saying. I stepped into the doorway, feeling like maybe Mom had a point. I figured it couldn't do any harm to listen. They were sitting in a circle, about a dozen of them, men and women of different ages. Some were like me, eyes cast to the floor, arms folded across their chests, but as my eyes passed across them, I was shocked to see someone I recognized leading the meeting, my old friend Clint.

We were pals at school, but we'd lost touch when we'd both gone into the army and been assigned to different units. It had been years since I'd seen him. We had been best buddies, and this was the last place I'd have thought to look. A smile flickered on my face, but I wasn't even sure if he would remember me. A lot of time had passed. I decided to stay in the shadows by the door, listening to a few other stories.

"You know, it's important to remember that we changed a lot while we were in the army but sometimes the people we come back to expect us to be the same. It's important to give them time to come to terms with how we've changed just as much as we have to come to terms with it. There's a big culture shock that happens when we return here. We've been living in another world, and there are a lot of things we've seen and done that the other people in our lives can't even begin to comprehend. One of the biggest gifts we can give ourselves and the people around us, is time," Clint glanced at his watch, "and speaking of time I think that's all the time we have this week. I'll see you all next week."

He rose and stood there, offering solemn nods and handshakes to the troubled people who came to him for help. They passed me as they walked out, looking at me with curiosity. I waited for them to pass by.

Clint still hadn't noticed me as he began to tidy up the chairs. I walked in and picked one up.

"I never thought you'd be one to give advice," I said. Clint was taken by surprise at the sound of my voice. He turned around, and a broad smile appeared on his face when he saw me. He opened his arms and hugged me tightly. I have to admit it felt good.

"Bobby, damn, I didn't know you were back. It's been some years."

"Just a few," I said. Clint looked the same as ever. He had the same tousled blonde hair and lazy smile, although instead of being clean-shaven, he displayed a dark shadow of stubble.

"You could have sat down. There's always room for one more."

"Maybe next time, I was just curious about what was going on here. I didn't expect to see you. How'd you get into it?"

Clint shrugged. "You know, when I got back, I heard a lot of stories about people who were struggling to adjust to being home again. I had my struggles as well; hell, I think we all do. I noticed a lot of people were hanging out here during the day and we started to talk and help each other. In the end, I just decided to make it an official group where people can come and talk about their problems, or just listen. It seems to help people, and it helps me too."

"Seems like it can get pretty heavy."

"It can, but it's good for people to get it out of their system. Some of these people don't have anywhere else to go or anyone to turn to. Look, the café here does some pretty good coffee, you want to grab a cup and catch up?"

"Sounds good me," I said without a second thought. There was a small café attached to the gym. A few people were sitting around eating their lunch. I didn't see anyone from the support group. Clint bought us a couple of coffees and paid for it without asking. I pulled out my wallet, but he told me not to worry about it because he got a discount for running the support group. We sat at a table by the window that looked out to the parking lot.

"So, what have you been up to all these years?" he asked.

"You know, this and that. I've been home for a few months now and it's...it's going well I guess."

"Oh yeah?"

"Yeah I mean, I'm just taking some time to adjust and get used to the swing of things. It's nice to be back in my own bed rather than some uncomfortable bunk."

Clint smirked. "You know, when I got back, I couldn't sleep in my bed. It was too comfortable. I threw my pillow on the floor because it was the only way that felt right to me. Some nights I still do it. I never thought the army would change me this much."

"I thought it would, but not in this way. I thought it would make me a better man."

"That's what was advertised, wasn't it?" Clint snorted a laugh. "Man you won't believe how many times I've wished I could run into the guy who approached us. I want to ask him if he was actually in the army or if he was just an actor."

"My bet is on the latter. I feel bad, like...everyone should know what they're getting into but the army keeps on recruiting people. It's like nobody listens to us and we're the ones that were out there. We're the ones who lived the life."

"I know, but people still want to serve. They have this idea that duty means doing whatever it takes for your country, but really we have a duty to ourselves, and the country has a duty to us as well. Somewhere along the way that got lost."

Clint sighed desperately.

"How long did it take for you to adjust when you came back?"

"I was lucky, I guess. It didn't take me long at all, but then again, I never really had to face what a lot of people had to face. I saw action, but I was never in any real danger. Sometimes I feel like a fraud; like I'm sitting there trying to help these people move on with their lives, but I don't really know what they're going through."

"You know more than most, and I'm guessing that they might need someone with a little objectivity. It's probably good for them..."

"It is. I've seen positive results already. What about you, are you staying with your Mom?"

"Yeah, for a while."

"I know how that goes. I'm staying with my Dad. It's...well...I'm sure you know what it's like. Some people aren't as fortunate as us. They don't have anyone who can take them in, and they're just lost in the system. You know what the main thing I've learned from all this? It's that the world is broken. There's just something fundamentally wrong with the society we live, and I'm damned if I know how it's going to be fixed. I look around, and it's like nobody cares that a lot of people are falling through the cracks."

"Do you know what you're going to do about it?"

Clint shrugged again and took a long gulp of coffee. "What can I do? I try and help people where I can, but I'm just one man. What can any of us do really?"

I mused on his words and thought he was at least doing more than I was. He was coming here week after week actually helping people while I was sitting in a sea of despair, losing myself to madness. I looked at him and found myself wishing that I had as much mental strength as him. He had always been the stronger one, probably because of what he had been through. When we were younger, he had been bullied, and I guess that had given him the kind of inner steel that was missing from me.

We sipped our coffee, and the silence became more tense. I suppose that always happens when you meet up with a friend after so long. It can't just go the same way as it did before. I remember we used to be able to chat shit for hours, but I guess the army robbed us of that ability as well.

"Do you want to go for a walk?" he suggested suddenly. I was taken aback by the offer, but I wasn't going to turn it down. There was a park nearby, so we tossed our coffee in the trash and walked away from the parking lot. We breathed in the fresh air, and I felt relief when we left the tall houses and wide roads, substituting them for lush trees and a sea of grass. Nature was calming, and as the birds sang and rustled the tops of the trees as they flew about, I felt much better.

"I love coming here, sometimes with a book, sometimes just to walk. You ever feel like you have too much time on your hands?" Clint asked.

"All the time."

"It's weird isn't it; when I was out there, I couldn't wait to get back home. I thought about all the things I missed and couldn't wait to do again, but when I got home, everything seemed so...hollow."

"I know exactly how you feel. Even watching movies isn't the same. Whenever I look around at the world, I see people who aren't like me any longer. I can't seem to connect with them. Sometimes I wish that we had our own place to live, so at least then we would know what we're feeling. There should be a program to help us get used to being in society again, not just throwing us back like a fish after we've been caught."

"They used us, abused us, and now we're left to our own devices," Clint said, squinting as he looked up at the sun. We walked along in silence. There was so much I wanted to say to him and yet it all seemed trivial, or too personal. We had once been the best of friends, but what were we now? I wasn't sure how to act around him. Part of me wanted to tell him all my deepest darkest secrets because I thought he was just about the only person in the world who would understand, but then I wondered if he'd even want that. He had to listen to people all the time when he led the support group. Talking about my problems was probably the last thing he'd ever want.

"In a weird way I miss it," he said.

I never expected to hear that. I looked at him with surprise and confusion in my eyes. He smiled and laughed a little.

"Maybe not that much," he added, "But I miss knowing what I had to do. I miss the routine and the missions, I miss the camaraderie. I had a lot of good friends." He bowed his head and exhaled softly. I wondered if he had lost anyone special, but I wasn't ready to ask him something so personal. There was something else I wanted to ask, something just as personal, and I wasn't sure I had any right to ask him it given how long it had been since we spoke, but he had once allowed me into his secret, a secret I hadn't shared with anyone. I wondered how many other people he had shared it with.

"How was it for you given...you know...?"

Clint glanced at me and nodded knowingly. "It was alright, actually. Things aren't as bad as they used to be. I didn't exactly go out of my way to tell people, but some suspected and others just guessed. I wasn't going to act like I was ashamed of it. Got into a fight once, but it wasn't serious."

"I'm sorry."

"Comes with the territory," he shrugged. "Most people didn't make a big deal out of it. There were a few other gay guys in the squad as well, so we stuck together. To be honest, it was good to not have to worry about what people thought of me. I was free to just be myself."

"So your Dad still doesn't know?"

Clint shook his head. I remember back at school when we had the conversation. We were just hanging out, and Clint had been acting weird, distracted. I figured he was just going through something, then out of nowhere, he told me he was gay. I didn't exactly react. It didn't mean anything to me; he was still my best friend. We carried on playing games. I'd always wondered if I reacted in the right way. But as soon as he told me he made me swear to keep it a secret, especially from his Dad. Hank wasn't the most liberal of men; his outlook was stuck a few decades behind the rest of the world, and he'd made no secret of his dislike for anything that went beyond his realm of normality.

It saddened me that Clint still hadn't been able to be honest with his father about this.

"I never thanked you for that day."

"You don't have to."

"No, I do," he looked at me earnestly. "You have no idea how nervous I was when you came to hang out. I wanted to tell you for ages, but I couldn't summon the courage. I tried to tell myself that there was something wrong with me, but in the end I couldn't deny the truth and telling you...damn, I was so afraid that you would up and leave and think I was weird and I'd be left with nobody to turn to."

"I hope you don't mean that. I think I was a better friend than that."

"You were," he said quickly, "it was just my paranoid mind. I was terrified, but you reacted perfectly."

"Really? I thought I might have been too insensitive or messed it up. I wasn't really sure how to react."

"No, it was perfect. It showed me that it wasn't a big deal in the grand scheme of things and that being gay wasn't the defining part of me; being your friend was. It helped me a lot, especially through my service. I remembered that, remembered that I was more than just a soldier. I had a life before the army, and I was going to have a life after it, as we all are."

"I'm glad I could help," I said, smiling genuinely. I felt a warmth in my heart in that moment, something that I hadn't felt for a long, long time. It was the satisfaction of knowing that I was doing something of worth in the world, that I was making someone happy.

"No worries. I'm glad I ran into you today, it almost feels like fate, doesn't it?"

"Something like that," I grinned. He checked his watch and told me that his Dad was expecting him to run a few errands, but we made plans to meet up again soon. Before he left, I called out to him and asked him if the support groups really work.

"They're not for everyone, but they do help some people. I think you get out what you put in. But Bobby, all of us can use a helping hand at some point, and we've got to look at the people around us. There's no shame in it," he said.

I was left thinking about his words and about everything I had experienced. I certainly felt better after having a conversation with someone other than my Mom, and I started to think that maybe there was a way for me to be happy after all.

Chapter 3

I returned home, and thankfully, there were no incidents with any potholes. I stopped off at the store to get some ice cream as a treat to go with dinner. When I returned, I smelled pot roast and tried to enjoy the feeling of home comforts. I dropped my bag off and then walked into the kitchen, where I put the ice cream in the freezer.

"How was your gym session?" Mom asked. I stopped for a moment and tried to remember what I'd heard in the support meeting about how you had to give the people you knew time to adjust, and I realized that I hadn't been very fair on my Mom. She had tried her best to accommodate and when I thought she was nagging me to do things like go out or go to a support group she was really just trying to reach out to me to make sure that I didn't lose myself in an abyss. I was lucky to have her.

"It was good. I...actually stopped by that support group you mentioned."

As I said this, she turned, and her eyes lit up.

"Oh, that's wonderful Bobby! How was it? Were there many people there?"

"There were a few, yeah, and funnily enough it's run by Clint."

"Oh, how lovely! You haven't seen him in a long time. How is he doing?"

"He's alright. Struggling along like the rest of us. We're going to hang out in a couple of days."

"That's good. It'll be good to get out with a friend. You've been so lonely recently," she said, smiling widely. Her eyes swam with tears. I hadn't realized how much my happiness meant to her until that moment when I saw the relief in her face, the simple relief of her son having a friend. I was about to leave, but I wanted to say something else. I wanted to tell her everything that was in my heart, although I was never good at sharing my emotions. Still, I thought it was important that I make the effort.

"Mom, I just wanted to thank you for letting me stay here and for putting up with me. I know it can't be easy. I know I'm not the son that you remember and-" She walked up to me and put a hand to the side of my face.

"Bobby, you don't have to thank me. I love you, and all I want is for you to be happy." She tilted forward on her tiptoes and kissed me on the cheek. It was a tender expression of affection, but one that had been sorely lacking for my life. It was the first time since I'd been home that I had opened myself up to something like that and it felt good, although it still felt as though I didn't deserve it.

The following few days were like most of the ones that had come before it, the only difference being that I had something to look forward to now. Hanging out with a friend was such a simple thing for most people, and yet for me it was a momentous occasion that was filled with anticipation and fraught with anxiety, for I wondered if us spending more time together would make us realize that we weren't as good friends as we used to be, and while it was fun to catch up we didn't have any bond that could continue into the future. I was worried about what to say and how much to tell him, but most of all I was worried that because we shared a history I would end up talking about what happened to me during my service and I wasn't sure I was ready for that.

But, when the moment came, I was eager to get out of the house. We went to the park again as both of us enjoyed being in nature. It was peaceful and calming, and for a couple of hours, we could leave the rest of the world behind.

"Have you kept touch with anyone else from school?" I asked as we strolled along the path. I reached up idly to pick a few leaves from some low-hanging branches. Nearby a fountain babbled, and berries glistened in the sun. Errant sticks cracked under our feet, and the tweets and caws of birds could be heard all around us.

"I tried to reconnect with a few when I got back, but it never really panned out. Most people we were close with made it out of here, and those who didn't aren't the kind of people I want to hang out with," Clint said. I pursed my lips and nodded. Most people wanted to leave our home town in the hope of chasing glory and opportunities elsewhere.

"You ever think you'll leave again?"

Clint blew out his cheeks. "I have no idea what's going to happen. I mean, I guess one day I'd like to, but Dad doesn't have anyone else, and I'd feel bad about leaving him here. I don't know where I'd go or what I'd do anyway."

"That's one of the hardest things I've found about coming back. I thought by now I might have a better idea of what I want to do with my life, but I'm just as confused as I was when I left. It all used to be so simple; we went to school, then the army, but now we're just supposed to know what we're doing."

"One of the hard truths I learned is that nobody knows what the hell they're doing in life. We're all just spinning around hoping to find some semblance of purpose, but a few of us get knocked back a little too hard."

"Do you think there's any hope for us?" I asked, trying not to let my voice crack with emotion.

"There's always hope, at least, I have to believe that. Otherwise, nothing we've been through is worthwhile. There's a lot of time left in our lives, and I choose to believe that there are always possibilities. I have to; otherwise, I don't know how I'd ever go on living."

We walked along in silence for a little while until we came to a grassy opening and we sat down, bathed in the golden glow of the sun. The air was sweet and warm, and as we lay down, I rested my arm against my face to shield myself from the blinding light of the sun. It was one of those idyllic days without any cloud cover in the sky. The grass was soft against my back, and I ran the fingers of my free hand along the ground, feeling the warm grass and the soft soil underneath. A few butterflies wafted around us, and I felt as though I just wanted to stay here forever.

"So what have you come up with when you've been thinking about what you want to be?" Clint asked.

"I honestly have no idea. I want to get a job, but the only ones I'm qualified for are ones that I should have been doing when I was a teenager. I've been thinking about maybe going into security, or even becoming a cop although I don't really want to put my hand on a gun again. Sometimes I get these flashbacks, and I feel as though I'm back in the war. It happens at stupid times, like the other day when I was going to the gym, I ran over a pothole, and I thought it was a mine. I don't want it to happen when someone else could get hurt."

"A lot of people go through the same thing. You should come to the next meeting; I think it would help."

"Maybe, although I don't think standing up and telling my story is for me."

"You don't have to talk if you don't want to, but it would be good to listen. And I'm always here if you just need a word."

"I appreciate that," I said, and then told him about the conversation I had with my Mom. He smiled widely and praised me for it, which made me smile too. I didn't realize how much his encouragement meant to me.

"Did you have a similar one with your Dad when you came back?" I asked. I figured since he seemed to have a solid hold on his feelings he might have been able to have that kind of conversation, but, from the way his head turned away and his long exhalation I knew that there was something wrong.

"Dad isn't really the type of person I can have those kinds of conversations with. He doesn't understand that my service wasn't filled with glory and honor, so when I try to talk with him about it, it just...well, the conversation never goes the way I want it to go. I think he wants me to be grateful to the army for giving me the opportunity to serve, and whenever I try to tell him how it affected me, he just brushes it off and says that I'll get over it. I can't tell him about what happened, or what I lost."

"Someone you knew?" I asked.

Clint nodded. "A guy. He was my...well, we were more than friends." He ran his hand over his jowls. "And I can't tell my father how important he was to me."

"How'd it happen?"

"The usual thing. He was out on patrol, and they got a lucky shot. Could have been anyone really, but it was him."

"I'm sorry. I lost people too. I can't help feeling like it should have been me. Like, why did I survive when they didn't? What makes me so special or deserving of life when they had lives too? No matter how much I think about it I can't quite get my head around that."

"That's "That's the thing ain't it. It's hard enough just to survive, never mind when you know that someone else could take your place and make a better job of it than you. The only way I can make peace with it is to believe that we have to live in honor of them and be as happy as we can be for their sake. I have so many mixed feelings inside. Without the army, I never would have met him, but also he wouldn't be dead if he never signed up."

"What was his name?"

"Jason. He was the first guy I properly fell for. When he died, I knew I had to get out of the army as soon as possible. What about you? Did you ever try looking Christine up?"

I let my head loll on the ground and let out a dark laugh. Clint propped himself up on one elbow and looked at me, his figure blocking out the sun, casting me in shadow.

"What's so funny? You two were good together."

"We were, and if I hadn't gone into the army, we might have been even better. There was one point when I was sure that we were going to get married and live the high school sweetheart fairytale."

"So, what happened?"

"She promised to wait. I told her not to, even though deep down I hoped she would. We spoke a bit while I was over there, and exchanged some letters. She said that she couldn't wait for me to get back home, but then when I did, she didn't make the effort to come and see me for a few days. Turns out that she had shacked up with Paul."

Clint's mouth dropped open. "Paul? Wait, Paul McCrae?"

"The very same."

"No way."

"I'm telling you, apparently after school, he went straight into working for this insurance place, and he got a few promotions. He owns a big house, and I guess that was enough to convince Christine that he was the man for her. They've got a kid on the way and everything."

"Wow, I guess nothing turns out the way you expect."

"You can say that again."

"So...is there anyone else on the horizon? You always did know how to catch the eye of a lady."

I smirked. "I think those days are long behind me. I've had a few conversations in bars, but I don't know, it just hasn't felt right. I haven't felt myself, and I don't want anyone else to get mixed up in this mess. When I sort out my own problems, maybe I'll start looking, but I don't think I'd make a very good boyfriend right now."

"I don't know about that, you're a good guy at heart, and when it comes down to it, that's what's important. Besides, sometimes to move on, you have to move on, you know what I mean? Like, you have to get back on the horse as soon as possible, or you'll forget how to ride."

"I think these things are like riding a bike. I'm not sure you can forget them. What about you, anyway? If you're so convinced that's the right way to live, why aren't you going out on dates all the time?"

"I said move on, not go and flaunt yourself to every available chick in the area. But no, unfortunately, the pickings are rather slim around these parts, which is another reason why I want to leave at some point."

"I'm sure there must be someone to play around with or ride like a bicycle," I said with a knowing smile and a teasing gleam in my eye.

Clint shifted his body so that his legs were folded and he leaned forward. He ripped up some grass from the ground and shredded it before sprinkling it back over the ground.

"You know, when I was younger, I thought all I wanted was to play around and experience as much as possible, and I thought maybe the army would give me that opportunity since I'd be away from home and away from Dad, but then I met Jason and everything changed. We just connected, you know, like he knew me better than anyone and I knew him, and I knew then that anything purely physical wasn't going to be fulfilling. I need the emotional connection, you know? I want to feel like someone really gets me, the same way he did."

"It sounds like you cared for him very much."

"I did...I do. It seems stupid because it's not like we were together for very long."

"I don't think it matters how long you're with someone for. Look at how many married couples are together for decades and just end up getting divorced because they were never really happy. The timing of these things doesn't matter all that much; it's more about the intensity of the feelings."

"Check you out," he nudged me in the shoulder, "maybe you should be the one to lead the support group if you're going to drop all these emotional insights."

I chuckled. "I wouldn't go that far, I just end up watching a lot of daytime TV, and I guess enough of it gets lodged in my mind."

"Well, you never know, you might be able to make a career out of it. I've been thinking about becoming a qualified therapist."

"That's really cool."

"Yeah, I like helping people at the support group. It's made me aware of just how many people need help, and how many people don't have anyone to talk to. Sometimes a conversation can do wonders, and I hate the idea of people out there struggling because they feel afraid or unable to talk to people close to them."

"It's weird the way that works, isn't it? How you can be afraid to talk to people close to you but feel comfortable to talk with a stranger."

"Just one of the many wonders of our beautiful brains," he said, and we both laughed. We continued enjoying the leisure of the park for a little while longer before we had to both leave, although in truth I would have happily stayed there with him until night fell. His company was a welcome respite from the loneliness I felt in my own company, and when I was with him, I found that I didn't have to be tortured by thoughts from the past. Before we went our separate ways, I pulled him back and thanked him for the afternoon.

"I was a little scared that we might have lost our rhythm. You know what it's like when people are apart for a long time. I'm glad that we can talk just like we used to."

"Me too," he said, "I can always use a friend. So, can I expect to see you at the next meeting?"

I thought it over for a few seconds and then nodded. "I'll be there," I promised, and I knew I wouldn't let him down.

Chapter 4

Over the following few days, I was in a happier mood. It felt good knowing that I had something to look forward to, and, although my nights were still plagued with terrors and there were occasions when I jumped at a car backfiring, I was overall in a better state than I had been in a long time. I tried to make more of an effort to spend time with Mom, even forcing myself to feign happiness in the hope that faking it would truly make it. I helped her with some jigsaw puzzles, and I knew that she appreciated the time we spent together, and that helped me feel a little better too. We didn't talk much. I guess she figured that if I wanted to talk about anything, then I would, and I doubted she wanted to hear all the gory details of my time spent in the army. There was something comforting about sitting in silence with her, knowing that she would always take care of me.

As the day of the meeting approached, I grew anxious and had second thoughts about going, but I didn't want to disappoint Clint. If I hadn't made him that promise, I may well have chickened out, but I steeled myself against this new thing and drove to the gym, making my way to the small room in the back where the chairs were set out in a ring. Most of the people there were familiar faces, but I was glad to see I wasn't the only new person. Clint gave me a warm smile as I entered and took my seat.

I hadn't planned to speak, so when Clint asked if anyone had anything they'd like to share my lips remained sealed. I looked around. A few other people seemed to share my reticence, but others were more used to the rhythm of these meetings. One woman stood up and wrung her hands together. I recognized her from the last meeting, but I hadn't heard her speak then.

"I'm Monica, for those of you who don't know me," she said. I noticed that she was always moving, even if it was just a twitch of her foot. "Recently I've been doing well. For those of you who are new, these meetings really do work. I've made so much progress, so much so that I started seeing a guy recently. We've only been together a few weeks, but it got me thinking about the future, and I couldn't help the way my mind just spun out. We were talking about our views on life, and the thing is, he knows I've been in the army, but he doesn't know the effect it had on me. And then we got talking about kids, and he said he definitely wants them, but I'm not sure if I do. How can I bring a child into this world knowing the kinds of things that go on? And I know that makes me strange because having a kid is a normal part of life. It's what we're biologically driven to do, but given everything I've been through…I wouldn't want that on them, and what's more, is that I'd want a child to be proud of me, but how could they be when I wouldn't be able to tell them about anything I did?

I thought I was ready to move on with my life, but when I think about the future there are so many things that fill me with doubt, and at the moment, I'm just wondering if I can go on and live a normal, fulfilling life."

She nodded and sat down, crossing her legs and bringing her hand to her mouth where she chewed on her fingernails.

Clint waited a few moments to see if anyone had any wisdom to offer Monica, but when nobody spoke up, he did.

"It's natural to have these feelings. Even people who haven't been through what we've been through feel overwhelmed with thoughts of the future. I think a lot of the time we have to put a hold on our feelings and take baby steps into the future. Our lives are long, hopefully," this raised a dry chuckle, "and the world is big. It's easy to get overwhelmed, but as long as we're happy and doing things that make us feel comfortable, we can feel assured that we're doing right by ourselves. I think as long as this relationship makes you happy, you should keep with it. People change over time, and as the relationship progresses, you might find yourself more at ease with the thought of having a family, but there's no rush and no pressure on yourself. I'd also suggest that you talk to your partner about these feelings. Honesty is one of the most fundamental aspects of a healthy relationship, and if he shares the same feelings as you, then I'm sure he'll want to help you through this, just like you'd want to help him if he was struggling with anything."

He spoke these words directly at Monica, but then he opened out his body to address the rest of the group in a wider point that he thought was applicable to all of them.

"You know, coming back to this life is scary in and of itself, and moving into a relationship is a big deal, but we can't let the fear control us. Being with other people is one of the few ways we can move on with life and give ourselves a good chance at happiness. We have to give ourselves that chance, but it also means we have to be vulnerable too. Sometimes we're going to fall for the wrong people, and they're going to hurt us, but eventually, we're going to find the right people, and they're going to help us through this mess we call life. Hopefully, we'll all be able to find trustworthy people who can help support us when we have moments of weakness and doubt, who can reassure us that everything is going to be okay, and who we can turn to for love and support. Monica, it sounds as though you've gotten lucky with this guy, so I hope that you can find the strength to share your feelings with him."

A few other people spoke throughout the meeting, and I listened intently. They all had different problems to share, but I noticed that everyone nodded along. We all understood their struggles. I had been feeling so alone ever since I returned, but here were kindred spirits, and the only question I had left for myself was why it had taken me so long to embrace the support of this group. However, I wasn't ready to share anything yet. I wasn't the only one not to speak, but I waited for Clint afterward, hoping that we could hang out. I helped him tidy the room.

"That was a good turn out today," I said.

"Yeah, the numbers fluctuate. Sadly a lot of the new guys won't return."

"How can you be so sure?" I asked, furrowing my brow in confusion. I figured that the hard part was in coming here, not in staying.

"That's just the way it goes. Support groups aren't for everyone. As much as I'm proud of the work I'm doing here, I'm not a professional, and some of them need more help than I can give. I feel bad that they're so alone they can't even bring themselves to reach out to us."

"I guess I know how they feel. I'm sorry for not speaking; I just didn't feel ready."

"It's cool, just go at your own pace. There's no pressure here. Some people have been coming for weeks, and they haven't said a word, but I'm glad they keep coming because it means it's doing some good."

I asked him if he wanted to hang out afterward, but he said he had a few errands to run around the house, so we could, but I would have to help him. I didn't mind that at all, so as soon as we finished clearing up the room we headed back to his place. His Dad didn't work much; he was a contractor, but work had been slim pickings for the last couple of years, so he was sitting in the lounge drinking a beer when we arrived. He welcomed me with a handshake and said it was an honor to meet a fellow soldier. I saw what Clint meant about his father having a different perspective on the army than the both of us.

We grabbed a sandwich before we went out into the yard and began to clear away some of the weeds that had grown in the garden.

"I was thinking about making this a little meditation area, a place where I can come to lose myself for a little while. I don't want to have to go to the park all the time just to relax," Clint said.

"I can't imagine your Dad would be happy at the prospect of having a meditation area. It doesn't seem like that's his thing."

"And you'd be right," Clint smiled. We got down on our hands and knees and began to rip up the weeds. It was surprisingly intense work. Before too long, our brows were prickling with sweat, and we needed some fresh lemonade to cool down. "Jason got me into it. He told me it helped him cope with everything that was going on."

"He sounds like quite a guy."

"He was…sorry, I don't mean to keep talking about him," Clint said and hushed his voice as he glanced towards the house, making sure that his Dad wasn't going to come out to eavesdrop.

"It's okay. I know you don't get much chance to speak about him. I'm sorry that I didn't get the chance to meet him."

"Me too, I think you would have liked him."

"So, you think Monica will take on board what you said today?"

"I hope so, and I hope the man she's with will give her the support she needs. But she's got a good head on her shoulders, so I think she'll be alright. At least she's taking her time with it."

"What do you mean?"

Clint paused a moment and clapped his hands together. Dirt trickled between his palms. "One of the biggest mistakes I've seen people make is that they jump into relationships as soon as they're back in the 'real' world," he added air quotes for extra emphasis, "when really they need time to come to terms with what's going on in their own heads. Sometimes it's not possible to avoid it because they've had partners waiting for them, but other times I think they just want to try and force themselves into living a normal life, and it never ends well. I get it, you know, sometimes it's scary to be alone."

"You can say that again."

There was a moment's pause.

"Are you alright, Bobby?"

"Yeah, why?" I asked, a little taken aback by his question.

Clint ran his hand through his hair as he looked at me. "I've seen a lot of people come back from the war. I know what it's like to be scarred and I just...I want you to know it's okay to talk to me. You haven't spoken much about your time over there, and I get that you probably don't want to relive it, but it does help to talk about it. I can tell you've been feeling some of the same things that the people in the support group were feeling. I want you to know that it's okay. I'm here for you."

My chest tightened, and my heart beat rapidly. My first instinct was to rise and flee, to run from the pain inside, but I quashed that desire and willed myself to stay sitting there. The truth was that I wasn't alright. I knew it, my Mom knew it, and Clint knew it too, but admitting it was another thing. I bowed my head and tore up another weed, enjoying the satisfying sound of the unwanted roots being ripped from the ground.

"I don't know anymore," I said.

"You mentioned that you lost people close to you. How many?"

"The whole squad," the words caught in my throat. It felt as though my mouth was filled with marbles.

"Damn. That must have been tough."

"We were just out there, and then there was an explosion. I was the only survivor. There was nothing I could do. I felt so helpless. Now every time I close my eyes, I'm taken back to that moment, and I'm forced to hear their screams again and again. They were my friends. And then I was left alone, and I can't do anything. I feel guilty because I'm not the son my Mom remembers. I feel ashamed because I can't just go out and get a job and earn money. I feel envious of everyone who is able to succeed at life without any difficulty, and I just feel so damned lonely," I looked up at him. My voice trembled with anguish and it seemed that as soon as I had started talking about my feelings and the difficulties I'd been facing, I wasn't able to stop.

"The worst thing about all of it is that I feel like it was for nothing. When I left, I thought I was doing the right thing. I wasn't ever any good at school, so college wasn't for me, and I wasn't ready to sit down and begin a career. I wanted to go to the army, develop my skills, and come back feeling proud; as though I had accomplished something. I thought it would put me in good stead for the future. Employers would look at me and see that I had done something with my life. My life would mean something, just like that damn recruitment officer told us, but instead, I've done nothing. It's like the time I spent in the army doesn't exist. I don't get to speak with my friends because they're dead, and I don't want to talk about what I experienced because it just makes me depressed and anxious. It was supposed to help me climb the ladder of my life, but instead, it just left me reeling, and I can't help but wonder what the point of it all was?"

"I wish I had the answers for you. I wish we had looked more into the army before we left so we could hear the truth, and I wish we had chosen another path. But look, Bobby, this is the path we're on, and we're the only ones with the power to change it. I know it's hard, and I know it feels like we're never going to match the expectations of the world, but we have to try and make our life worth something because we're the only ones with that power. I hate that we have to fight just to be happy and sane, but it's a fight we have to win, and you're going to win it. I know you will because you're one of the strongest people I know," he said, taking my hand and clasping it tightly. I felt the power of his words, I felt the strength of his faith in me, and I felt confident that I could do it. I nodded, wanting to make him proud, wanting to be the person he saw in me.

"It's going to take time, but we'll get there, together," he said.

"Together," I promised. It was as though we were teenagers again, making grand promises about life that we tried to keep, but they were the promises of youth.

"You ever think ten years ago we would end up here?" I asked.

"Hell no, but here is where we are, and at least we're together again. Hey, you want to bust out the PlayStation and play some games once we're finished up here?"

"Sure thing, as long as it's not a shooter."

WE FINISHED UP WITH the weeds pretty quickly and then returned indoors. Clint called out to his Dad and told him we were done and were going to hang out in his room. His Dad muttered something from the couch, engrossed in whatever he was watching on TV. When we got upstairs, I was a little surprised at how familiar it all was, especially Clint's room. He even had some of the same posters up. When I pointed this out, he laughed, a little embarrassed.

"I'd much prefer to have posters of shirtless men, but I don't think my Dad would appreciate that. I can't wait until I get a job or something so that I can finally leave this place and have my own space. All I want is a little bit of independence," he said.

"I hear you, but thankfully, Mom lets me have a lot of freedom, and she never comes into my room without knocking."

Clint had closed the door, so we didn't have to worry about being quiet. We settled on his bed as he set up the game; we decided on a racer just to let our adrenaline fly, and we laughed when we crashed.

"I seem to remember being better at this game when I was younger," I said.

"Your reflexes were sharper then," he said as he overtook me. I pressed the controller hard, trying to urge my car on with my willpower. Tires screeched as I drifted around a bend, but there was no catching him, and he burst across the finish line with flames trailing from his exhaust. He threw down the controller and whooped with delight.

"I forgot what a sore winner you were," I said dryly.

"Come on, let's do another one. I'll go a little easier on you this time," he said, picking up his controller. This time he let me pick the track. It didn't help. I lost that race and the next, but it was still fun, and it took me back to a time when nothing else mattered, when the only thing we had to worry about was a little bit of homework. The game was fun, but what was more fun was hanging out with Clint. We jostled each other as we raced and pushed into each other. We laughed just like old times, and I felt a real connection with him. It was as though he was the only person in the world to truly know me, both parts, the version of me that used to be and the me that had returned from the war.

Eventually, we decided to take a break from racing, and after we settled down, I revealed something intimate about myself.

"You know, I feel like you're the only one I can talk to about everything I've been through," I said.

"That's because we know each others' secrets. We know each other even better than we know ourselves."

"And we've shared everything."

"Not everything."

He looked at me in a strange way, and then suddenly, his hand was on my cheek, and he leaned in to kiss me. His lips brushed mine; I was so shocked that I didn't have a chance to pull them away. I couldn't believe it was happening. The moment stretched out into forever before I pulled my mind back and stood up. I wiped my mouth and looked at him in shock and surprise.

"What are you doing?" I asked.

He pushed himself back onto the bed and held up his hands in apology.

"I'm sorry, Bobby, I must have read the wrong signs. God, man, I'm sorry. Please don't leave. Let's talk about this."

I didn't want to talk. I didn't want to do anything. I stormed downstairs and walked out of the house without even calling out goodbye to Clint's Dad.

Chapter 5

I was still in shock when I returned home. I checked my cell, and there weren't any messages waiting. I almost expected one from Clint to try and explain what had happened. Had it really occurred the way I remembered? I tried to tell myself that I had made a mistake, that something had crossed wires in my brain and I was just imagining it, like the way I had imagined a pothole was a mine, but I knew that I was only trying to lie to myself.

It had happened. Clint had tried to kiss me. After all our years of friendship, he'd made a move, and I had run away. Why, why had he done this? What signs had I given him? I just wanted him as a friend; at least, I thought I did. Hell, I wasn't even gay! He knew that. He knew that I was straight, so why was he trying to put this on me? Why did he kiss me?

I threw myself onto my bed and put my fingers to my lips. The soft warmth of his lips lingered against mine. I closed my eyes and remembered the way his mouth had brushed against me, how he had cupped my cheek tenderly in his hand...I stopped myself. This couldn't be happening. I wasn't gay. I mean, I had no problem with it at all, but it wasn't who I was. I liked women...but part of me liked this as well.

Clint and I had always gotten on well, and it was satisfying feeling emotionally attuned to him, but it didn't sit right with me. We were just friends.

God, I was so confused.

I lay back in bed and tried not to think about him kissing me. I told myself that we could just move past it and not bother to acknowledge it, but I knew that could never happen. Pandora's box had been opened, and we could never go back to a time when we hadn't kissed. I had so many questions, and maybe I should have stayed there to talk to him about it, but I needed space. Now I didn't know if I could see him again. I was awkward and embarrassed, and I didn't know how to handle this situation. He was the only friend I had left, and he had to go and do this. I just needed someone to talk to. I just needed someone to be there for me, but he'd kissed me, and now everything was ruined.

I turned around in bed and tried to stop my heart from beating faster when I thought of him kissing me. I tried not to let my mind wander and think about what could have happened if I hadn't gone away. I tried not to think of his sexy physique and his lazy smile and how easy it was to be myself around him. We'd both spoken about the need for intimacy and the need to feel at ease with another person, about being able to be honest with them and feel comfortable when sharing emotions, and there was nobody I felt more at ease with than Clint, but this was all new and unreal and I was…I was straight! I liked girls. I got off on girls…so why couldn't I stop picturing him and me kissing?

I yanked my pants down and started to fondle myself, forcing myself to think of girls, beautiful, busty blondes with long legs and curves in all the right places. A smile settled on my face as a haze drifted through my mind, and I relaxed in what was a familiar position. My hand found a good rhythm as my erection throbbed and grew to its full height and thickness. The veins rippled under the taut skin, and I grunted softly as my body sang with desire. I clamped my eyes shut as my mind became vivid and vibrant, the images taking on lives of their own. I thought about the girls all surrounding me, a busty bevy of beauties all wanting to pleasure me. My back arched as I tightened the grip around my cock, and then suddenly they all disappeared, and Clint was standing there, topless, his muscles glistening with sweat after a workout. His pants were open, and a narrow line of hair pointed down to his crotch. He smiled at me, and his eyes gleamed with desire. I groaned as I opened my mouth and he put a finger against my lips before he pressed his mouth against me once again, drowning out my protests, muffling my claims that this wasn't what I wanted because God it felt so good and I couldn't stop thinking about him at all. I thought about his hands roaming over my body, about the way his taut skin would feel when pressed against mine. I remembered the taste of him on my lips and imagined our tongues dancing together. It was as though the gates of my soul had opened, and this desire came pouring out. I didn't know if I was gay or bi or whatever, all I knew is that thinking about Clint made my body burn with arousal.

I pumped hard and fast, my hand moving to a steady rhythm as I pulled it forward and backward, feeling my entire body tense. Breath caught in my throat as I twisted my head from side to side. This was so wrong, and yet it felt so right. I kept trying to tell myself that I shouldn't be feeling these things, but I just couldn't stop myself. He was the only thing in my mind. Even when I tried to force myself to think of women, they all just dissipated like a fine mist, leaving only him standing in my mind, looming above me, the promise of searing desire settling over my tingling skin and then it came in one hot supernova of passion. My mind cracked, and I felt the warm liquid seep over my fingers and stomach. I groaned long and hard, and my head lolled to the side. I tried to deny myself this was happening, tried to say that it didn't mean anything, but it did. It meant everything.

It meant I wanted Clint.

I QUICKLY WALKED TO the shower and lost myself in the warm water. I watched it cascade over my body as I leaned against the tiles and put my head directly under the shower, letting the water blur my vision. My mind reeled with the intensity of the orgasm. It was the most satisfying one I'd had in a long time, and it was all because of Clint. I'd never thought of him like that before, but something had changed. Maybe this was normal? Maybe this was something that happened to people after they came back from a war? I was left with questions, and I had no idea how to answer them. The only person I could really talk to about it was Clint, and right now he was the last person I wanted to face.

When I got out of the shower, I checked my cell, and I did notice that I had a message from him asking for me to call him. I told myself that I'd do it later, although I was pretty sure that I wouldn't be able to. Speaking to him now, just seemed wrong. I needed to sort things through in my head first. I needed to figure out what I was feeling.

The following few days were difficult. Mom noticed a change in me and asked me if I was going to be hanging out with Clint again. I told her that it was unlikely because he was busy with a few things. I couldn't bring myself to tell her the truth because I wasn't even sure what the truth was myself. Clint was my friend, my oldest friend, but that was all. He wasn't someone I thought about romantically.

I tried to keep busy and forget about what had happened. Part of me was glad that Clint hadn't tried to call again or come round, but another part of me wanted him to. I was lost at sea without any idea of how to handle this situation. I tried to think about it logically at first. Even though Clint seemed to be holding it together, he was still upset about his lover Jason, and maybe he had been craving romance. It was probably just his loneliness that had prompted him to take such an action. He had confided in me before, and as he'd said, pickings were slim. I probably shouldn't have held it against him, but he'd sent my mind spinning, and I wasn't sure if I could see him again.

Days passed and it soon came time for another support group meeting except for this time I wasn't sure if I was going. Mom asked me the night before, and I told her that I wasn't sure I was getting too much out of it. She looked disappointed, and I wished I could have told her the truth, so she didn't think I was just giving up on it. But Mom was an insightful person and had her own kind of wisdom.

"Did something happen between you and Clint?"

"Why do you ask?" I shot her a suspicious look. I didn't want anyone knowing about the kiss we shared.

"It's just that you seemed so excited to be hanging out with him again, but this week you've seemed a little more down-hearted, and you haven't been out as much. I know you're not the same little boy that used to have disagreements with his friends, but you're still my son, and I know how you think."

I gave her a wry smile. I shouldn't have been surprised that she was so wise when it came to me, but I was still slightly taken aback. I wasn't ready to tell her the truth even though she probably would have been okay with it. Unlike Clint's Dad, Mom had never said a bad word against anyone and always believed that people should mind their own business and do whatever made them happy, as long as it didn't cause other people harm.

"Have you ever had a situation where somebody has done something that completely surprises you? And you're not sure if you can see them anymore, even though you still have a lot in common, and you could probably still be friends, but it's going to be really awkward, and maybe things aren't ever going to be the same afterward?"

Mom had a coy smile. "I've had something similar to that, yes."

"How should I handle it?"

"Well, I suppose first I would wonder if what happened is worth sacrificing a friendship for. People are never going to do what we always expect, just as we're always going to do things that surprise them. So we have to give them a bit of slack and accept their mistakes just as we hope they're going to accept ours. You and Clint have been friends for a long time, and it would be a shame to see that end over something that a conversation could fix, which leads me to my second point, and that's about what kind of person you would like to be. Do you want to be the kind of person who runs away from these problems and doesn't try to talk them through with people you know? Do you want to be the kind of man who is too afraid to face your feelings and to explain the way you feel?"

"No, I don't," I said definitively.

"Then I suppose you know what you have to do," she said, placing her hand upon mine. "Bobby, life is long, and if we stopped speaking to everyone who annoyed us or made a mistake, then we'd all be very lonely people. Forgiveness is one of the most important qualities to have, and even if you give someone the benefit of the doubt and you end up being hurt, you can at least console yourself with knowing that you did the right thing. All that being said, I still don't know what exactly happened between you and Clint, so you have to make the judgment call about whether you're willing to give him the chance to explain himself."

I thought about her words for the rest of the night. I barely slept, so consumed was I with this conundrum. I eventually realized that I was avoiding Clint because I was scared to accept that I might actually want to kiss him. It was all so new to me, so shocking, but Mom was right; I didn't want to give up on the only friendship I had because of this. I didn't want to throw away years of history just because he found me attractive. I had reacted well when he'd come out to me, but this time I knew I had reacted poorly and I could only hope that he didn't hold this week's silence against me.

THE FOLLOWING DAY I rose and composed myself for the support group, telling myself that it wasn't going to be a big deal and it was all going to be okay. I thought about just going to the tail end of the meeting, but figured that would be more awkward, so I left with plenty of time to spare, but there was a small accident on the way and traffic was delayed, so I was a little late. I burst into the room, and all eyes turned to me, and I saw how surprised Clint was to see me. His gaze darted away almost immediately.

The meeting was good, although I found it difficult to concentrate on what people were saying because I kept thinking about Clint. He didn't look at me once after I entered the room. When the meeting was over, I stayed. It had become a routine for me to help him with the chairs, but this time he turned his back on me.

"Clint, I just came to talk about what happened."

"It's okay," he said without turning around to face me, "I think we can both agree that it was a mistake and we don't need to talk about it. I'm...I'm sorry for doing that. It was a mistake, and I misjudged the situation. Clearly, you were disgusted, and I understand if you don't want to see me anymore, I'm just...I'm sorry for doing that. I overstepped my bounds, and I obviously misinterpreted what was going on. I'm such a fool. I guess my loneliness got the better of me. I wish I could take it back."

"I don't," I said, my words blunt and clear. That was enough to get his attention. He turned around and looked at me with disbelief in his eyes. I licked my lips and swallowed, trying to rid myself of the lump in my throat.

"What do you mean?"

"I...I don't know. But I was shocked when it...when you kissed me. I wasn't expecting it at all, and I'm sorry for ignoring you this past week, and for running away. That wasn't very mature of me. I was just surprised, that's all. I wasn't disgusted." I stepped closer to him. I noticed him getting tense. Now that we were alone in the same room together, I realized how much I had missed him. The light shone on him in a way that made his eyes glow, and I found myself drawn to him powerfully, like a moth to a flame. My gaze fell to his lips, and all I wanted was to feel them against mine again.

"I don't know what's happening to me," I said, talking through my thoughts as they entered my mind. "I'm not gay, but you awakened something in me. When you kissed me...I couldn't stop thinking about it afterward. I tried, but you're there, in my mind. I can't stop thinking about you, Clint. I don't know what this is supposed to mean, but it wasn't a mistake. I'm not willing to let our friendship die over this."

"I don't want that either."

There were two chairs that hadn't been put away yet. Clint sat down in one, and gestured for me to take a seat.

"Have you always felt like this?" I asked, wondering if it was going to cast a new light on our friendship, but Clint shook his head.

"Don't take this the wrong way, but you were always just a friend and I would never have done anything to jeopardize that. I guess with the time we spent apart seeing you again was different. When you told me that you felt like you could share anything with me I knew how you felt. To me it felt as though we were moving beyond that. I felt a pull towards you and I just couldn't stop myself. I'm sorry for getting you mixed up in this, I'm just a mess."

"I don't think you're that bad, you've got a pretty good handle on things from what I can see. I don't think you could help this many people if you were a mess."

Clint leaned forward and placed his head in his hands. He looked up to make sure that nobody else was in the room and looked aghast.

"I feel like a fraud. I preach all these things, but I can't follow them myself. I'm not doing as good as I led you to believe. I can't stop thinking about how lonely I am. I sit in my house day after day with a father who doesn't even know me. I come here and I'm the leader, but I never feel like it. I only felt myself when I was around you. I'm still messed up over Jason's death as well and I don't know if I'm ever going to get over him properly. Being with you reminded me what it was like to be with someone and I couldn't stop myself from reaching out. I know it's not what you want. I shouldn't have deluded myself that anything was going to happen. I know you're not gay, and it's okay, you don't have to treat me with kid gloves. I know what I did was wrong."

I listened to him and pity swelled in my heart, but the whole time I couldn't stop thinking about the kiss, and I knew that I wasn't feeling these things out of a sense of pity. The feelings I felt were genuine, although confusing.

"How...how did you know you were gay?" I asked, my head bowed.

"I don't know it's just...it's just something inside. But look Bobby, you don't have to do pretend. It's kind of you, really it is, but I know you're not like me."

"Maybe I am...something inside me has changed. I don't know what it is. When you kissed me, I was shocked and scared. I didn't know how to feel about it, but the more I think about you the more I'm attracted to you. I don't know how to make sense of it myself. This is all so new to me."

"How do you want to proceed?" he asked, his voice trembling with nerves. I knew how he felt. Part of this felt wrong, like it wasn't me, at least the me I was used to being, but as I looked into his eyes it felt right as well. It felt as though I belonged right there, with him.

"I'm not sure I've...I've never done this before. I wasn't sure how this conversation would go."

"I wasn't expecting to see you again. I thought for sure I had ruined our friendship."

"I guess this is just another level to our friendship. I guess...do you want to go and grab a drink or something?"

"I think a drink would be good," he said, and we both smiled.

Chapter 6

We drove into town and found a bar that was deserted at that time in the afternoon. The lights were low and we ordered a couple of beers. The sports channel was showing highlights of last night's baseball game and there were a couple of people shooting pool. We picked a table in the corner and sat down. I still felt awkward. Clint was my friend, a man I'd known for years, but this felt as though I was meeting him for the first time. We laughed nervously and sipped our cold beers.

"So, come here often?" he drawled, and we both laughed again. "I know you probably can't answer this, but do you have any idea why you've changed? Like, is this some latent thing that's always been hiding under the surface, or did something happen when you were in the army that awoke this side of you?"

I searched my mind, hoping that there was some key to unlock this mystery, but I couldn't find one defining moment. I shook my head. "I really wish there was because it would make the whole thing easier, but I never even fantasized about it until you kissed me."

"Well, I guess I should take it as a compliment that I was able to bring out this side of you. Maybe being gay is a superpower after all. I guess you're seeing the world in a whole new way. So who are your big crushes? For me, it's got to be Captain America. He's one soldier I would sign back up for."

"Actually that's the funny thing, this sounds really corny, but it's only for you."

"What do you mean?"

I had a sharp intake of breath and looked around. I wasn't used to talking about this kind of thing at the best of times, let alone when these feelings and sensations were all so new to me. I had gotten used to being a discreet person, and although I knew rationally that Clint wasn't going to judge me, I still felt like I was under the microscope. Talking about these things made me vulnerable, and that wasn't a feeling I liked to experience.

"Okay, so when I first realized that I might like this kind of thing, I sort of decided to test myself, so I thought of a few different things and I realized that it wasn't the men I liked so much as it was you. It just didn't seem to work unless it was you. So I'm thinking that maybe for me it's not so much that I'm attracted to men or women, it's that I'm attracted to the soul inside or the emotional connection, or some deep shit like that." I took another long sip of beer.

"I guess it makes sense. We've both been lonely. It's more difficult to find people who can identify with us now, and it's not going to get any easier as time goes by."

"When I think about it, it does make sense. Like, when I found out that Christine had gotten married and that she'd led me on, it just changed the way I felt about her. The emotional bond had been broken, and so had my attraction to her. It all evaporated instantly, kind of in the opposite way to how my attraction towards you happened. Can you tell me about Jason?"

"Are you sure you want to know? I mean, if we're going to start something here do you really want to know about the guys in my past?"

"I think it's good to know. He obviously meant a lot to you and you haven't been able to talk about him with anyone else. I'd like to know about him."

Clint nodded. "He was...he was just a good person. He was kind. He always had time for everyone and tried to make the world a better place through his actions. He was humble, he minded his own business and the only thing he ever wanted was for everyone to be happy. Sometimes I wondered why he even signed up to the army because he was so gentle and tender. He used to take care of the animals on the base. There was this scrawny looking mutt, really the most pitiful and pathetic thing you had ever seen. His fur was mangy and he was probably ridded with disease, but Jason saw something in that dog. He shared his rations with the animal, and soon enough we were all sharing our food with him. That was just the effect he had."

"How did the two of you get together? Like...did you both know you were gay?"

"I think we both sensed it. We were paired together a lot and we got to talking. I had a crush on him from the first time we met, but I thought he was way out of my league. One night when we were all watching a film we were sitting together and I felt his hand creep onto my thigh, his fingers reaching out to mine; at first I thought there must have been some sort of mistake so I froze and withdrew my hand, but he rested his on my leg and squeezed it. I looked up at him and saw him smirk, so I put my hand on his and we stayed like that for the whole movie and then, well, we went back to his bunk and we let out all the tension that had been building between us."

"Did you have to keep it a secret?"

"It was an open secret, but nobody really minded. We just had to make sure that it didn't interfere with his duties. We both tried to keep each other grounded, telling ourselves that we shouldn't get too carried away because anything could happen. We'd heard horror stories, but even then it didn't seem like that was us. There were nights when we talked about what we'd do when we returned home. It always felt like we were having forbidden conversations, which I guess made the whole thing more exciting. We had a lot of plans together. We just couldn't stop ourselves, and then it all changed. I didn't even get to say goodbye properly because there wasn't enough left of his body. There was so much unfinished business between us. A lot of the relationship was lived out inside my head, you know? Like...we didn't really get a chance to go on a lot of dates so I always imagined what our lives would have been like if we made it back here, but then all that was taken away from me before I was ready."

"That's rough man." I reached out a hand and placed it upon his. His skin was warm, his flesh rough after all the handiwork he'd been doing in his house. He nodded somberly and stared into his beer.

"Are you sure you want to try this with a messed up guy like me?" he asked, his eyes tinged with sadness.

"You're a hot mess," I joked, trying to lighten the mood. "But look, this is all so new to me as well. I'm happy to take things slowly. Let's just spend time together and explore this thing. There's still plenty that I need to learn, and I think we're both pretty vulnerable at the moment, but we've known each other for long enough that we can trust each other with our feelings. I know I wouldn't feel confident about expressing this with anyone but you."

"That means a lot. I'm glad you feel safe with me, and I'm glad that you are happy with me talking about Jason."

"Have you ever considered coming out to your Dad?"

Clint snorted. "I've thought about it yeah, but I don't think it's a good idea. I just don't see a way he's going to understand, and I really don't need the hassle of being thrown out of my home for what I am. I think it might be one of those secrets I keep until my grave."

"It can't be good, holding onto something like that."

"No, it's not. Jason thought I should tell him as well. He was of the opinion that I shouldn't have to hide myself, not even from my Dad. Maybe if I had my own place to live I'd be a little braver, but I've seen how quickly things can go to shit for people. There are so many people who haven't had a support network like you and me, and they're left to fend for themselves; except they can't, so they end up on the streets and once you're out on them it's almost impossible to get back on your feet. I just can't risk it."

"I get that. Did he have the same problems with his parents?"

"No, he was out and proud. He said they had known since he was young, so he never had to worry about them not understanding. I was always envious of him for that. Sometimes I wonder what it would be like if I just walked downstairs and announced to Dad that I'm gay. Sometimes I think that he would be so shocked he wouldn't even bat an eye and just carry on as normal, but then I hear the way he talks about people on TV, and how he cusses and curses and I know that he'd just see me as a failure."

My heart went out to Clint. I hadn't been able to grasp the pain he'd been through during his life, and all I wanted was to make it better, but I wasn't sure how. I wasn't as confident or composed as Jason and I knew I would never compare as a lover because I had never been with a guy before, but I knew that wasn't important. This wasn't a competition. He had loved Jason dearly, and Jason had been taken away from him, just like my friends had been taken away from me. We had both lost so many people. I was suddenly filled with the urge to tell him all my secrets, to lay my soul out on the line and give him a window into my psyche.

"When I came home I wished that I had died with the rest of my squad because I knew that it would have been easier. I couldn't sleep because I couldn't stop crying, and every day I've been feeling so guilty for my Mom because it's like her son did die out there and only a ghost came back. I never wanted to die before, but it sometimes it seems like it's the only way."

"You have to find something to live for," Clint said. "You should share this at the meeting. There are people there who want to help, good people, and by sharing you can make a difference to other people too. Maybe it's okay that two broken people like us can get together."

"Saves us from making other people's lives a living hell," I smirked. There was a lot of dry humor that pervaded our conversation, and I honestly wasn't sure where this was going to lead or what we should say. It almost felt like we were just trading sob stories with each other.

I had to ask myself what I wanted out of this. Was it just someone to commiserate with, someone to share lamentations with while we thought about how much our lives had changed, or was it because I wanted a fresh start and to believe that there could actually be something like hope waiting for us?

I pulled him up by the hand, leaving our half-empty glasses standing on the table behind us. I took him outside where the bright sun hit our eyes, a stark contrast to the dim, dark interior of the bar.

"Where are we going?" he asked.

"Somewhere fun," I replied with a smile on my face. I took him to a nearby putt putt course where we had a lot of laughs. I realized that it was dangerous for us to talk too much of what we had lost because it would only make us dwell on it. We had to start looking at the future and enjoying the time we spent together.

Around the end of the course, I gave him a high five when he sank a hole in one after making an impossible shot through the cannon on a pirate ship, and I told him my thoughts.

"This is what's important. We have to help each other move on," I said.

"It's a deal," he replied, and we finished the course and walked back after getting some ice cream. The hours had passed in a blur. Suddenly dusk was setting in and the pale moon peeked out from behind a misty cloud. We were walking close together and our hands fell into each other, our fingers entwined. We smiled at each other. Ever since we left the bar we hadn't spoken about the war, the army, or anything we had left behind, and it made me feel normal again.

It was with sadness that I walked to my truck because I didn't want the day to end. When I expressed this thought, he looked at me with sympathy and told me that there would be others. We hugged, and the hug turned into a kiss. We were both still tentative. I suppose he was afraid that I would pull away again, and I was afraid that I wouldn't like it as much as I had before, that I was only leading him on through my confusion, but as his lips touched mine fire rose inside me and my arms reached around him tightly. I pressed my body into his and felt his heat simmering in the air around us. Our tongues fought for dominance, and my mouth was filled with his sweet taste. His hot breath washed against my lips, and I gasped as the intense sensations surged through me.

When the kissed ended I staggered back a little, dazed, and he seemed to take great enjoyment in this.

"I'll give you a call tomorrow and we can do something else fun. Today was great," he said. And it was. I got in my truck, and I missed being in his arms immediately. When I arrived home, Mom was waiting for me and gave me a wry smile. I wondered if she knew how close me and Clint were, but I wanted to protect his secret.

"I take it you made up with Clint?" she asked.

"I did. I took your advice and realized that I was just overreacting. His friendship is more important to me than anything else. We spent the day together and it was good."

"Just like old times?"

I tilted my head as I considered her words.

"Not exactly, but I think that's okay. We're never going to get our old times back. We just have to appreciate the time we have together."

I went up to bed and reflected on the day, wondering why I had been so hesitant before. If there was one thing I had learned from my time in the army, it was that we shouldn't let ourselves miss out on good times because we were haunted by the past. I had already seen firsthand how easy it was for everything to slip away, and Clint had experienced it as well. There had been a lot of hurt in my life, and maybe it was that trust that was the defining factor in my attraction for Clint. I knew that he wouldn't let me down, and that he wouldn't judge me for being myself in front of him. I could share my darkest secrets and know that he wouldn't shy away, and I hoped that he knew the same was true of me.

Over the following week we spent as much time together as we could, and yet it still didn't seem to be enough. We strolled in the park, went to the arcade, drove around town, took in some movies, and hung out at each other's houses. We never ran out of conversation, and I was the happiest I had been in a long time, as was he. It felt as though a weight had been lifted from my soul. It hadn't been easy to open myself up to something like this, and although it didn't erase the pain of the past, it certainly gave my mind something else to focus on. I began to think of my time in the army less and less, especially before I went to bed. Instead of remembering the deafening explosions, I thought about Clint and what the two of us were going to do the following day.

While we were outside, we were affectionate with each other, but we wanted to keep it a secret from the other members of the support group. It wasn't a conscious decision, as in we didn't talk about it with each other, but as soon as we were at the gym, we walked along side by side without holding hands. I didn't want our happiness to overshadow the group since there were people there who didn't have the same fortune as us, but more than that, I didn't want Clint's authority to be undermined by others knowing that we were involved. I still wasn't confident enough to speak, so I listened as always, but this time I paid more attention to what Clint was doing, and how he earnestly listened to everyone who spoke to him. He was calm, patient, and kind, and in that hour, I grew more attracted to him than ever. As we were packing the chairs away, I was filled with the overwhelming urge to grab hold of him and kiss him. I started to tear off his clothes. My desire was rampant, and I didn't think there was anything that could stop me from having him, but he pushed me away, a wary glance focused on the door that could swing open at any moment.

"Not here," he gasped as I leaned into him, trying to coax more passion out of him. These desires were so new and unfamiliar to me that it only added to the excitement, but I was also nervous and knew

I would need to strike while the iron was hot, so I didn't lose myself to feeling overwhelmed. "Anyone could come in."

"Kinda makes it a little more exciting," I tried to tease, but Clint wasn't having it. He turned away from me, and I started to think that maybe there was more to it than just him not wanting to get interrupted. Although we'd held hands and been physical, and cuddled up to each other, things hadn't progressed beyond that stage. I had been happy because I wanted to take things slow, but I noticed how he tensed and became resistant when things became hot and heavy. I knew that I couldn't hold in my passion for much longer.

"Is everything alright?" I asked.

"Of course, I just don't want to be interrupted."

"Or maybe there's something else. Is this about Jason?"

"What do you mean?"

"Like maybe you're not as over him as you thought. Maybe you're not ready to be intimate with anyone else. It's okay if you're not, I just hope that you can do me the decency of being honest with me, because right now I kinda feel like when we get close we become even further apart, like you're pulling away from me just when we should be getting more intimate."

"It's not deliberate," he said. I didn't want to be jealous of Jason. I wanted to be the bigger man and not be insecure about things like this, but I couldn't help but feel like there were three people in this relationship, and I was quickly becoming the least important one.

"Then what is it? At the moment I can't help feeling like I'm a substitute."

"It's not about Jason!" he said, his voice rising. I was taken aback by the force of his words and realized that I had touched a nerve.

"Then what is it? I'm not angry, I just didn't expect you to be so hesitant. You're the one that's done this before; I figured you'd be the aggressor. I didn't expect to have to be the one to initiate things. Am I doing something wrong?"

He looked at me for a moment. His face was aghast as he seemed to come to a sudden realization. He put his hand to his head and rubbed his temples, closing his eyes for a moment. Then, he stepped towards me and looked pained and regretful.

"I'm sorry Bobby. I didn't realize I was making you feel like this. When you said you wanted to take it slow I suppose I didn't realize how my actions might come across as being distant. I should have been more sympathetic to your needs and desires."

"That's all well and good, but what is the problem here if it's not Jason? Because I can't think of anything else!"

"It's this place."

I looked around, puzzled why the hall would bleed out into the rest of our relationship, but he quickly corrected me.

"I don't mean the hall Bobby, I mean this town, this country," he almost spat out the last word. "All my life, I've had to put shackles on myself to stop myself from being who I am so that my Dad doesn't find out. I had to pretend to be someone else for him, and I got used to pretending so much that I'm not sure how to fully release myself. Out in the army, I could be myself without worrying about what he'd think of me. I guess just taking that last step means I'm going to have to confront him sooner rather than later, and I don't know if I'm ready to do that yet."

"You won't have to do it alone," I said, taking his hand and giving him a soft kiss on the cheek. He smiled at me and opened his arms, taking me into his body, sharing his warmth with me and kissing me deeply. I moaned with contentment as I melted into the kiss. It was becoming second nature to me now, and I couldn't believe that I had ever shied away from the wonders of his kiss. I was hungry to taste more.

"Speaking of Dad, he's out with his buddies tonight. Why don't you come round?" he asked. A grin appeared on my face, and I nodded eagerly as my anticipation rose through the roof.

Chapter 7

I had a shower and got ready, spraying some musky aftershave around my body. I wore a light blue shirt with the top two buttons undone, and some jeans with a leather belt tied around my waist. My heart raced while I prepared for this date, as I was going to do something I had never done before. It reminded me of my first time with Christine. I was a bundle of nerves back then as well, but somehow this seemed more important and unique. I drove my truck to his house, and as I walked up to his porch, I inhaled deeply and rapped my knuckles against the door. He opened it, and he looked gorgeous. He wore a similar outfit to me, but he wore it better.

"You smell great," he said. So did he. We kissed as I slipped into his home, and the kiss didn't end when I thought it would. He grabbed my collar and we twisted through the room, until he slammed me against the wall, making the pictures rattle. The embrace was breathless and soon he dragged me up the stairs. I stumbled, barely able to catch my footing, and then suddenly we were in his room, and the door slammed shut. Everything was a blur. His hands were all over me; his mouth was locked to mine as we unleashed all our passion. I was swept up in the whirlpool of desire. The bed creaked as we fell onto it, his body was on top of mine, hot and heavy. His hands tore at my clothes, running under my shirt, against my scorching flesh. I felt my arousal swell, and I almost felt as though I was going to come there and then. My hand reached down, my fingers dug into the tight denim that wrapped around his thigh, and I squeezed. He grunted and I could feel his manliness pressing into me. I grunted as I drew my hand up and groped his crotch, my eyes rolling into the back of my head as I felt his arousal. The air was sizzling and sweat prickled all over my body.

Tingling sensations ran down my spine and bloomed out all over me. His hand reached behind my head and brushed the back of my neck, causing a flutter of emotion to sweep over me. I rolled him over and fumbled with his belt, while his hands caressed my back and tore open the rest of my buttons, leaving my shirt hanging off my shoulders. He roamed around my torso and rested his hand against my beating heart as I struggled with the metal clasp, wanting and needing to get to what lay in wait for me, to what my body craved.

All the while we exchanged fervent kisses. A haze rose in my mind, and the world became blurred. I began to lose all sense of time and space, forgetting where I was. The only thing that mattered was his body and the sensations that were swimming through my burning blood. The room was filled with our grunts and groans. I squeezed the outline of his erection and finally managed to undo the metal clasp that held it all together, I opened the jeans and pulled them down, revealing his huge erection. My mouth hung open in awe, and I reached out tentatively, almost afraid to touch. The moment my fingers met his taut flesh with the rippling veins my heart almost jumped out of my chest; I had only ever felt my own cock, so it was surreal seeing my hands massage another.

Clint threw back his head as the pleasure washed over him, pleasure caused by me. I shifted my position so that I was curled up next to him. I rested one hand on his stomach, tracing a circle around the thin black hairs that rested around his navel, and with the other, I explored his erection. I squeezed and massaged him, and ran my thumb over the smooth mushroom tip. I followed the path of the pulsing veins to the bottom of the shaft and then cupped him in my grip, pumping softly and slowly, before increasing the rhythm as I noticed how it made Clint's head move from side to side in ecstatic anguish.

"You're a natural," he breathed, and I felt it was high praise coming from such a sensual, erotic man.

His hand fell to my head and started to twine through my hair. I felt a little pressure on my scalp as he moved me closer and closer to his erection. I looked up at him, meeting his gaze with my eyes, and I swallowed my nerves.

"It's okay," he whispered, and leaned his head back as I let him push me forward, and I opened my mouth wide. My lips met his erection and stretched over his thick shaft. Heat filled my mouth as did the musky taste of his sex, and I had never experienced something so delicious in my life. One hand curled around the base of his shaft, holding the throbbing organ steady as I let my saliva drip down and coat it in foamy liquid, while the other reached up and stroked his stomach and chest, feeling his powerful body be rendered moaning and writhing underneath the power of my mouth.

Eventually, it became too much for him to bear, and he pushed me off, kissing me eagerly, burning me with his mouth. I groaned as we twisted around the bed. He pushed me onto my back and shifted his position so that his legs were near my bed, his huge erection coming near my face. I reached out and grabbed it, holding it in place so I could feast on it again, sucking it long and deep, and then I felt him pushing down my jeans and underwear, taking my erection in his hands. It was the first time I had ever been touched by another man. He was strong yet tender, powerful yet loving, and I let out a long groan of pleasure.

He sucked me in the same way that I was sucking him; we echoed the sensations of each other. I was lost in the heat of his thighs. Our bodies were entwined in such a way that it became impossible to know where one of us ended and the other began. Our arms wrapped around the backs of our thighs, and I felt his hot flesh burning underneath my fingers. His tongue swirled, and he took all of me in his mouth, which made my entire body tremble. I could feel the tension rising within myself, and I knew it wouldn't be long before I came, and that was the moment when Clint decided to pull his mouth away.

He sat up and put his arms around me, holding me close. For a few moments we stayed there, breathing together, enjoying the calm silence that hung between us. We kissed tenderly, for our mouths were sore, and we could taste each other on our lips. We traced lines down each others' bodies, gazing with awe and delight. For the army, our bodies had been trained to be perfect weapons, honed to be used for destruction and all our physical perfection had only been forced upon us so that we would be able to fight well and perform our duty. But we had been left behind, and now our bodies became something else, something beautiful. I didn't see a soldier when I looked at Clint. Instead, I saw a beautiful man who glowed with an ethereal erotic energy, an energy that I found both addictive and intoxicating. I pressed my fingers against his chest, his hips, his thighs. I even found the innocuous areas of his body fascinating and alluring, although, in that moment, my eyes were always drawn back down to his rigid erection.

Clint touched me in the same way, caressing the side of my face and drawing his fingers along my mouth. I caught his thumb and began to suck it, nuzzling my head into his neck. He wrapped a strong arm around me and held me close. I felt his heartbeat thrum through his body and passion pulse within him. He ran his fingers through my hair, and we kissed again. I wanted him so much I thought I was going to explode. I clawed at him and whimpered helplessly, unable to process all the intense and overwhelming sensations running through my mind. It was as though I was a virgin again, an inexperienced teenager who didn't know how to handle himself when with another person.

But Clint knew how to handle me.

He gripped the back of my neck and forced me down to my back. My head nestled in the pillow.

"Now let me show you what this is all about," he said, smirking as he let his lips hover inches away from mine, tantalizingly close, his breath and mine mingling in the air, dancing away as his right hand traveled slowly down my body. Breath caught in my throat as I felt his hand slide around to my hips, fingers digging into my thigh. I assumed he was going to play with my erection again, so my eyes shot open when his hand went past and stroked a part of me that had never been touched before. Waves of intense pleasure rocked me, and I almost pushed him away, such was the shock of the intimacy. I stared at him, uncertain and a little scared.

"It's okay Bobby, I know what I'm doing. Trust me, just let the pleasure wash over you. Your life will never be the same after this," he said, putting his fingers in his mouth and licking them so that they were dripping wet. Then, he put his hand into the dark shadows caused by the close proximity of his body and I clamped my lips together, enjoying the pleasure that came with his long, curious fingers finding the secret sweet spots of my body, parts of myself that I had never known existed.

Ripples of pleasure tingled and swept through my body like a wave of electricity. Clint went slow and gentle at first, but soon he curled his fingers deep and circled my sensitive rim. He used his thumb to fondle my balls and stroke down the joining passage, the dark valley where everything seemed to be heightened. My head rocked side to side and my eyes clamped shut. I gasped and moaned loudly, unable to stop myself. My blood boiled, and my arms clutched him tightly, for I didn't know what to do with myself. My body was just an instrument of erotic delight, and Clint seemed to know how to play me perfectly.

Then, suddenly, he drew his hand away, and I found myself disappointed. I looked at him, wondering why he had stopped, but then it became clear to me. He kissed me softly as he adjusted his position. I felt the tip of his erection slide against my thigh as he shifted himself so that he was right against me. He circled his tip against me, and I arched my neck, ready to take him. I nodded, begging him, wanting him more than I had wanted anything else in my entire life.

Inch by thick inch, he slowly entered me, stretching me, showing me a whole new world of pleasure. I was so overwhelmed that every ounce of strength I possessed faded from my body, and my arms fell by my side. A guttural moan rose through me as I felt him fully inside me. He reached right into my very soul, as though he filled me completely, and I was empty without him. I thought I was going to faint from the utter bliss that blanketed my mind, but then he began to thrust and my eyes shot open. His arms cradled me and his terse moans blasted against my face. He kissed me intermittently, but I was lost in his masculine scent and his sheer power. I lifted my hands to rest on his back, feeling the primal movements of his strong body as he thrust into me. He seemed to get deeper and deeper with every thrust until I thought he was going to split me in two. He seemed to lose himself in the moment, becoming a sheer force of erotic energy. I took him and welcomed him, and I soon lost myself as well. My thoughts became an incoherent mess, and I grabbed onto the back of his head, forcing himself deeper into me. I wanted him to go faster; I wanted him to show me everything I had been missing. He pounded me hard, drove me into the bed. Sweat trickled down the valleys of my body and my moans turned silent, so overwhelmed was I by everything he was giving me.

I felt the pleasure rise inside me. I clawed at him, but before I could tell him what was happening, it took me by surprise, and I exploded, unable to stop my body expressing its desire. My mind cracked and everything around me went hazy as I felt the wetness slide down my stomach and crotch. He groaned loudly too, my cum smeared against his stomach, and that was all he needed to push his ultimate desire through. The sensations accelerated through my body and propelled us into a fast and intense orgasm. His body convulsed and shook, and when he came, it was with a loud roar. I felt him empty himself inside me; warmth spread through me in a fiery blaze, filling me up.

A broad smile lingered on my face as I let my arms fall by my side. My head lolled back, and I basked in the afterglow of passion. Clint stayed inside me for a few moments longer, twitching and tense, kissing me softly as his heartbeat settled. He smiled at me and then eventually extricated himself, handing me some wipes that he kept in his drawer so that we could clean ourselves. We nestled into each other, kissing each other lovingly.

"So, how was that?" he asked.

"Just wonderful," I replied. I knew then that I didn't want to be anywhere else. I leaned against his chest and stroked his body, feeling completely fulfilled and satisfied. I wasn't sure I had ever experienced that much pleasure in one moment, and now my mind was clear of all doubts. I wanted to be with Clint totally, completely, and utterly. My mind, body, and soul were all his, and I wasn't going to be able to live without him.

I laid in his strong arms, and everything seemed like it was going to be alright.

But then we heard footsteps outside, and suddenly the door flew open. We looked at each other, panicked, as we flung the bed sheets off and tried to make ourselves decent, but before we could, his father was standing there, his face the picture of disappointment and confusion.

Chapter 8

His expression turned from one of confusion to utter contempt. He snarled at us. Clint sat bolt upright, and I clung to the sheet, using it to hide our modesty.

"What the hell is this!" he yelled, jabbing an accusing finger in the air. "I knew there was something wrong with you. All this time living in this house and you've been...this," his face twisted with derision. "I'm going back out, and when I come back, I don't want you here."

He slammed the door behind him. I turned to Clint, who looked utterly shocked. His face was as white as a sheet, and he just stared at the door where his father had just been standing.

I had no idea what to say.

I put my hand on his shoulder and squeezed it gently. So much pleasure and passion had evaporated. Now a funereal atmosphere hung around the room.

"I'm sorry," I said.

"So am I," he croaked, and then rose from the bed. He moved numbly, more like an automaton than a man, as he got dressed and sighed. He pulled out a duffel bag from underneath his bed and started to throw some clothes in.

"What are you doing?" I asked.

"I'm doing what he said. I'm getting out of here. I don't want to be somewhere I'm not wanted. I always knew this day was going to come eventually. I should have known that he was going to react like this." His voice was devoid of emotion, and that worried me more than anything. He should have been angry. He should have been furious, but instead, he was merely accepting it as though it had always been inevitable. I reached out and grabbed his hand, trying to get him to stop for a moment and look around at what was happening.

"Clint," I said, "stop. You can't just accept this. It's not right."

"It's his house, his rules."

"But you have a right to live here too! You can't just let this happen."

Clint glared at me. "All my life he's been saying these things, and I was stupid to hope that he might actually see me differently. It's my fault really. I should have left a long time ago. Maybe this is what I needed. Maybe I just needed to be pushed out," he said.

"It's not your fault at all," I squeezed his hand supportively. "You shouldn't ever have to feel bad about who you are or what you want out of life. Your Dad has to come to understand that. And what are you going to do? Where are you going to go?"

Clint shrugged. "I'll find somewhere. People like us always do."

"No. I'm not having you living on the streets and slipping through the cracks. You're worth more than that, Clint. You're a good man, and you've been helping people. You have ambitions in life. You actually want to be something. You can't let this ruin you. You can stay with me for a while, at least until you and your Dad work through this."

"Don't you understand? He's never going to work through this. This is just who he is, and as much as I'd love him to change and accept me for who I am, it's just not going to happen." He looked despondent, and I didn't know if there was any way I could get through to him. "And are you sure that you're ready to reveal this secret to your Mom? If I stay with you, I don't think we're going to be able to keep this from her."

I thought about it for a moment, but only a moment. "I am," I nodded firmly. "I'm not ashamed of this, of who I am. My feelings for you are real Clint, strong and deep. I'm still not sure I fully understand the scope of all this, but I want to explore them with you. You're important to me, and I want my Mom to know that. I'm not going to let you be alone now. We need each other, more than ever."

"You're a sweet man Bobby," he said, placing his hand upon my cheek, but my words didn't seem to have had any effect. Clint continued to move around his room, filling up his duffel bag with all his belongings. When he was finished, he looked down at it and turned towards me. "It's pretty pitiful that my whole life can fit into this bag." Tears followed his words. I approached him and opened my arms to him, holding his sobbing, shaking body. I wished that I could take the pain away and make his Dad see the same thing that I saw, but in this, I was powerless. All I could do was be there for him to the best of my ability.

"Why aren't I good enough for him?" he bemoaned, and I didn't have an answer for him.

"Your whole life isn't in that bag, Clint. You're more than the things you own, we both know that, and I'm sorry your Dad can't see it, but I do. You mean so much to me. You've saved me. I don't know what I'd be like without you." I had no idea if my words were getting through to him, but I needed to say them anyway. Emotion swelled in my heart as I held him, feeling like I wanted to protect and take care of him against all the world's ills. I realized then that our roles had reversed. Instead of him protecting me, it was me protecting him, and I knew then that we were going to take care of each other. "I...I love you, man," I said. The words sounded a little hesitant at first because I wasn't sure if it was too early to say, but I meant it. Love had many different dimensions, and I loved him in so many different ways. I loved him romantically and as a friend. I loved how he took care of me, and I loved how he was vulnerable. I couldn't imagine anyone not loving him, and I hated his father for how he had reacted.

We stayed there on the bed for I don't know how long. Time didn't seem to be that important to us. He mumbled back that he loved me as well, but I could tell his mind was on other things. The future was uncertain for him. We both knew what the world was like for veterans like ourselves, how it was merciless, and opportunities were few. Without a good job, he couldn't afford an apartment, and although I was sure Mom would take care of us, I didn't want to be too much of a burden on her. It was bad enough that she had to put up with me; I didn't know how long she could take having to put up with the both of us. He'd have to go on the street, and once you were on the street it was difficult to get back. He had ambitions, and it seemed wrong that the revulsion of a father could ruin his life.

Eventually, he rose and wiped his eyes. A couple of hours had passed without us being aware of it.

"We should go," he said. "I don't want to be here when he comes back."

"You know this isn't the end of it. Maybe you two can talk it out; maybe he just needs to get used to this." I was trying to be hopeful, but I could tell that I wasn't managing to convince either Clint or myself. He just looked at me without saying anything. I knew he didn't believe that his father could change.

It must have been hell for Clint; spending his entire life pretending to be someone he wasn't, always living in fear that his father would disown him, and then when he finally found someone who accepted him it ended in tragedy. I was hoping to be his happy ending, but would he be able to be happy here, always being reminded how his father had shunned him and thrown him out?

I picked up the bag and walked out with him, but as we were about to leave, his Dad opened the door, and there was a moment of panic when they saw each other.

"It's okay, I'm just leaving," Clint spat. "But before I go I want to tell you something I've wanted to tell you for a long time. This is who I am, Dad. I've always been like this, and there's nothing wrong with it. When I was in the army, I fell in love, and he was taken from me before his time. I was happy, and the war took it away, and now I'm happy again. I love Bobby. I loved him when we were younger, and I love him now. I loved him as a friend, and I love him as a romantic partner, and

I feel sorry for you that you'd rather see me unhappy. The problem with you is that-"

"Sit down," his father said quietly, seething. I stepped back. Part of me wanted to defend the man I loved while another part knew I should have been respectful and not gotten involved in the family dispute. I swallowed my fear, hoping that the emotional anguish wouldn't rise and turn to violence.

Looking at them was like looking at the same person but in a mirror. Clint's Dad was older, his close-cropped hair was tinged with silver and his broad shoulders were accompanied with a rounded belly; the athletic figure was still there underneath the flab that came with a life spent on the couch with a beer in hand, but I wouldn't have wanted to go toe to toe with him. The man was still intimidating, with his sun-bleached skin and throbbing veins on his temples.

"Sit down!" he yelled, and pointed to the lounge. "You're still my son, and you'll do what I say."

For a moment I thought Clint was going to strike him, but there was some part of him that still respected the authority of his father. Perhaps it was that part of us that was trained by the military to accept authority figures, or maybe it was just the piece of us that had been taught since birth that our parents had the final say in our lives. Clint slumped his shoulders and walked past me into the lounge.

"You come too," his Dad said as he passed me. I followed and remained beside Clint. I didn't know what his father had planned, but I didn't like it one bit. I stood beside Clint and placed my hand on his shoulder. The duffel bag was still in my hand. I let it rest on the floor, although I was ready to pick it up at a moment's notice if anything went wrong.

I was curious about what Clint's Dad had to say. He paced across the floor before descended into his armchair like a king into a throne. An empty beer can toppled over at his feet, and there was a clear indentation where he spent most of his days. In many ways, this wasn't a man anyone should have respected, but he was Clint's father, and that gave him a measure of respect.

"I've always...suspected you were different. When you didn't show an interest in girls, I figured that something was different inside you, but I thought it might just be a phase that you would grow out of. I was proud when you joined the army. I thought that it would straighten you out and make a man out of you. I've been proud of what you've been doing with the support group. I'm proud of you for helping others, but what I saw tonight..." he winced. "It's nothing personal Clint, but you know I'm an old-fashioned man. Some things are normal now that weren't normal when I was growing up. The world is changing, and sometimes that makes it a scary place for an old coot like me. I'm used to things being a certain way, and when I see that it just...it took me by surprise is all."

"What's the point to all this, Dad? Are you really going to try and tell me that you've had a change of heart? Come on, I know you better than that. This is just a waste of time. I don't want to be somewhere I'm not wanted so let's stop pretending this is anything other than what it is. Let's just agree that I'm not the son you wanted and move on with our lives. I think it's the only way we're going to be happy. Maybe we don't need to be tied by blood anymore."

Clint's Dad looked subdued.

"I'm trying to explain so you'll understand. Maybe you're not the son I wanted, but you're the only son I have...dammit," he scowled and looked contemplative, as though he was trying to pluck the right words from his mind. I felt a little pity for him then; he clearly wasn't used to talking about emotions. I knew how difficult it could be to crack open that shell and talk about the really important things. It was only with Clint's help that I had been able to express and face my own emotions.

"When I left tonight, I went back to the bar. I spoke about what had happened. I was angry, confused. I thought my friends would understand, but then we all got to talking. A few of them have lost sons in the war, and the only thing they told me was that I should be grateful I still had my son in my life, because life hasn't been the same for them ever since they lost their boys. And I realized they were right. I can be stubborn and pig-headed, and sometimes I say things I regret, but never think for a second that I don't love you. I've only ever wanted you to be the best person you can be. God knows I'm not perfect. I'm make mistakes. I know I'm not always going to say the right thing or act in the right way, but you can be damned sure that I'll always do right by you because you're my kid. You're the only family I have, and I know that I'm lucky to have gotten you back.

I'm sorry for not handling this in the way I should. I don't want to lose you."

There was a moment of silence before Clint spoke.

"So, you mean you're not kicking me out?"

"Not yet," his Dad said with a wry smile. "Eventually you're going to have to leave though. I don't want to walk in on that again." He looked at me, and I flushed with embarrassment, turning my head away.

"I appreciate you making the effort, Dad," Clint said. He rose from the chair, as did his father. They walked towards each other and gave each other an awkward hug. I decided to make a timely exit to give the two of them some time to repair the chasm of emotion that separated them. I kissed Clint on the cheek, not wanting to flaunt our relationship in his father's face, and then returned home by myself where I told Mom all about what had happened. Thankfully she was happy for me and only wanted me to be happy.

And I was.

It felt as though I had finally turned a corner. After all the nights of anguish and haunted terrors, after so long of living in the terrible moment that I thought would define my life, it seemed as though I was finally ready to move on. I was at the beginning of a relationship with my closest friend, and I knew this one was going to last. It was still new to me, but it was exciting as well.

Clint and his father still had plenty of issues to work through, so we decided to keep our relationship low key while we were at his place, but we still managed to steal plenty of moments of passion together. I couldn't get enough of him. He quickly became my whole world, and the only thing I wanted was to make him feel good. I swiftly became a natural at pleasuring him, and we became experts in each others' bodies, becoming intimately familiar with each others' secret sweet spots.

We continued to attend the support group and helped other people try to find the same kind of peace and happiness that we had found, although there were times when I still had nightmares about losing my squad. But, when I did, Clint was always there to help soothe the nightmares away. He applied to train as a therapist, and after much thought, I decided to get off my ass and go down to the police station to see what it would take to train to become an officer of the law. I knew I wanted more from my life than to have a menial job. There had been a reason I had enlisted in the army in the first place. I wanted to protect and serve, so it seemed natural that I should become a cop.

When I first returned home, I used to look back at the decisions I made and wish that I could return to my younger self and slap him around the face, telling him not to be so stupid as to sign up to the army. I wanted to tell him about all the horror and pain, but I realized that everything happened for a reason. If it weren't for those decisions, those mistakes, I would never have been willing to open myself up to the emotions that Clint had shown me. When I signed up for the army, I thought I would become a man, but really it had only shown me what I shouldn't be in life. It showed me the chaos and relentless misery of war, it showed me how easy it was for people to be forgotten and left behind, and it showed me that you should never put your country or your duty above your happiness. The only thing that should come before you were the people you loved because, at the end of the day, they were the only people who were going to care about you.

I had been through a rough journey, but I had managed to find a good path. Now when I looked towards the future, I saw a brilliant highway illuminated by hope instead of a dark void promising nothing but misery. Clint and I spent a lot of time with my Mom and his Dad, and our emotional bond only grew. I don't think his Dad was ever going to fully accept Clint's lifestyle, but as time went on, he became more comfortable and accepted that his son was the way he was. He even came to some of the support group meetings to talk about his experience as a parent whose child went to war and all the difficulties that went along with that, and there were some surprising revelations about his views on the military, and how he too, had to evaluate what his country meant to him.

In time, Clint and I discussed the future and what it held for us. We decided that we wanted kids, so we started to discuss adoption, and we agreed that we wouldn't hide our experiences from them if they asked. Our job as parents was to teach our kid the difference between right and wrong, and we wanted more people to know about the truth of the military.

I never did track down that recruitment officer who lied to us and sold us on a dream that didn't exist. But I always knew exactly what I would have said to him, and I was going to say the same thing to any kid that thought about a career in the military. I would tell them to think twice, because what you bring back from war is a whole lot heavier than what you take with you, and unless you get lucky, there's not going to be anyone to help you carry the weight.

I never believed in the war I was fighting as a soldier, but as a cop, I had faith that I was doing the right thing, and I could see the difference I was making in my home town. I got to go home to a gorgeous, loving man every night, and, slowly but surely, my time in the army became a distant memory.

Enjoy what you read? Please leave a review!

Don't miss out!

Visit the website below and you can sign up to receive emails whenever Van Cole publishes a new book. There's no charge and no obligation.

https://books2read.com/r/B-A-RTRV-RGSYC

BOOKS2READ

Connecting independent readers to independent writers.

Did you love *My Soldier*? Then you should read *Off The Ice*[1] by Van Cole!

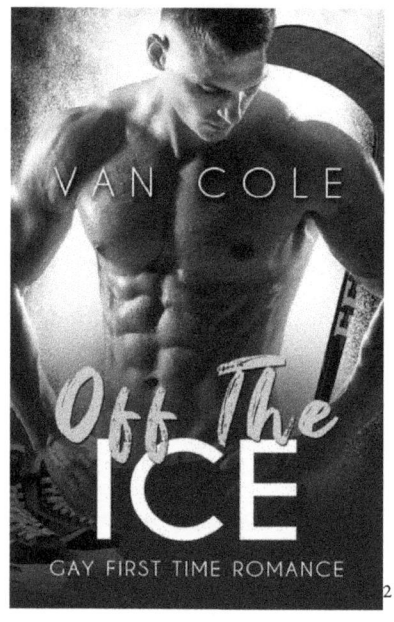

Chris Knoll is one of the top players for the New York Rangers. Anybody who knows anything about hockey is impressed with his performance – and that includes noted sports journalist Matt Tucker. Trouble is, not everybody in the industry takes Matt too seriously because he's openly gay. When he arrives to conduct a profile of Chris for Sports Illustrated, Chris's homophobic teammates are quick to warn him to be careful. As the two get to know each other, however, Chris's guard goes down and his interest kicks in. Despite the backlash against him, Matt is tenacious and bold. He defies all the negative stereotypes Chris has ever had about gay people – and he's awakening an attraction in Chris that's never come to the surface before. But for

---

1. https://books2read.com/u/mgY6nD

2. https://books2read.com/u/mgY6nD

a top-league sports player at the height of his career, swarmed by girls every time he leaves the house, hooking up with a writer is not really an option. After all, this is the kind of secret you try to hide from journalists. What are you supposed to do when a journalist is the secret? What's more, how are you supposed to square that with your intensely judgmental best friend?Only one thing's for sure. Chris doesn't have a choice. Whatever happens, he's just going to have to run with it.

Off The Ice is a standalone Gay Romance with a HEA and NO cheating!

Also by Van Cole

3 Man Huddle: MMM Best Friend Romance
His Alpha Wolf: Gay First Time Romance
A Dragon's Miracle: Gay Dragon MPREG Romance
Double-Teamed: MMM First Time Football Romance
His Football Star: Gay Second Chance Romance
Love In My Town: MM First Time Romance
Training A Hockey Star
Game Night
Double Shift
Take A Shot
Dear Professor
Getting Inked
Ninth Inning
Triple Threat
Seducing My Best Friend's Brother
My Protector
The Blueprint
Show Me The Way
End Zone
Matched To His Tiger
Love At First Puck
My Straight Boss
Falling For The Alpha
My Boss
On Thin Ice

Going Offside
Loving Luke
Fix Me
Off The Field
Falling For My Tutor
Off The Ice
My Soldier

Milton Keynes UK
Ingram Content Group UK Ltd.
UKHW011834120424
441050UK00001B/71